D0547555

HOPE

AND OTHER URBAN TALES

Hope and Other Urban Tales is Laura Hird's second collection of short stories. A previous collection, *Nail and Other Stories*, was published by Canongate's Rebel Inc imprint, and she followed it with her widely acclaimed novel, *Born Free*, which was short-listed for the Whitbread First Novel Award and nominated for the Orange Prize. Two other novellas appeared in the anthologies *Children of Albion Rovers* and *Rovers Return*. Her stories have appeared in publications throughout Europe and the USA. She lives in west Edinburgh.

Also by Laura Hird

Nail and Other Stories

Born Free

MORAY COUNCIL
LIBRARIES &
INFO.SERVICES

20 19 64 38

Askews

F

HOPE

AND OTHER URBAN TALES

LAURA HIRD

CANONGATE
Edinburgh · New York · Melbourne

First published in Great Britain in 2006
by Canongate Books Ltd,
14 High Street, Edinburgh EH1 1TE

An earlier version of 'Hope' originally appeared
in the anthology *Rovers Return* in 1998 by Rebel Inc,
an imprint of Canongate Books Ltd
Copyright © Laura Hird, 1998
'This Is My Story, This Is My Song' originally appeared
in the anthology *The Hope That Kills Us* in 2003 by Polygon
Copyright © Laura Hird, 2002

1

Copyright © Laura Hird, 2006
All rights reserved

British Library Cataloguing-in-Publication Data
A catalogue record for this book is available on
request from the British Library

1 84195 573 6 (10-digit ISBN)
978 1 84195 573 5 (13-digit ISBN)

Typeset in Garamond by
Palimpsest Book Production Limited,
Polmont, Stirlingshire

Printed and bound by
CPD (Wales) Ltd, Ebbw Vale

www.canongate.net

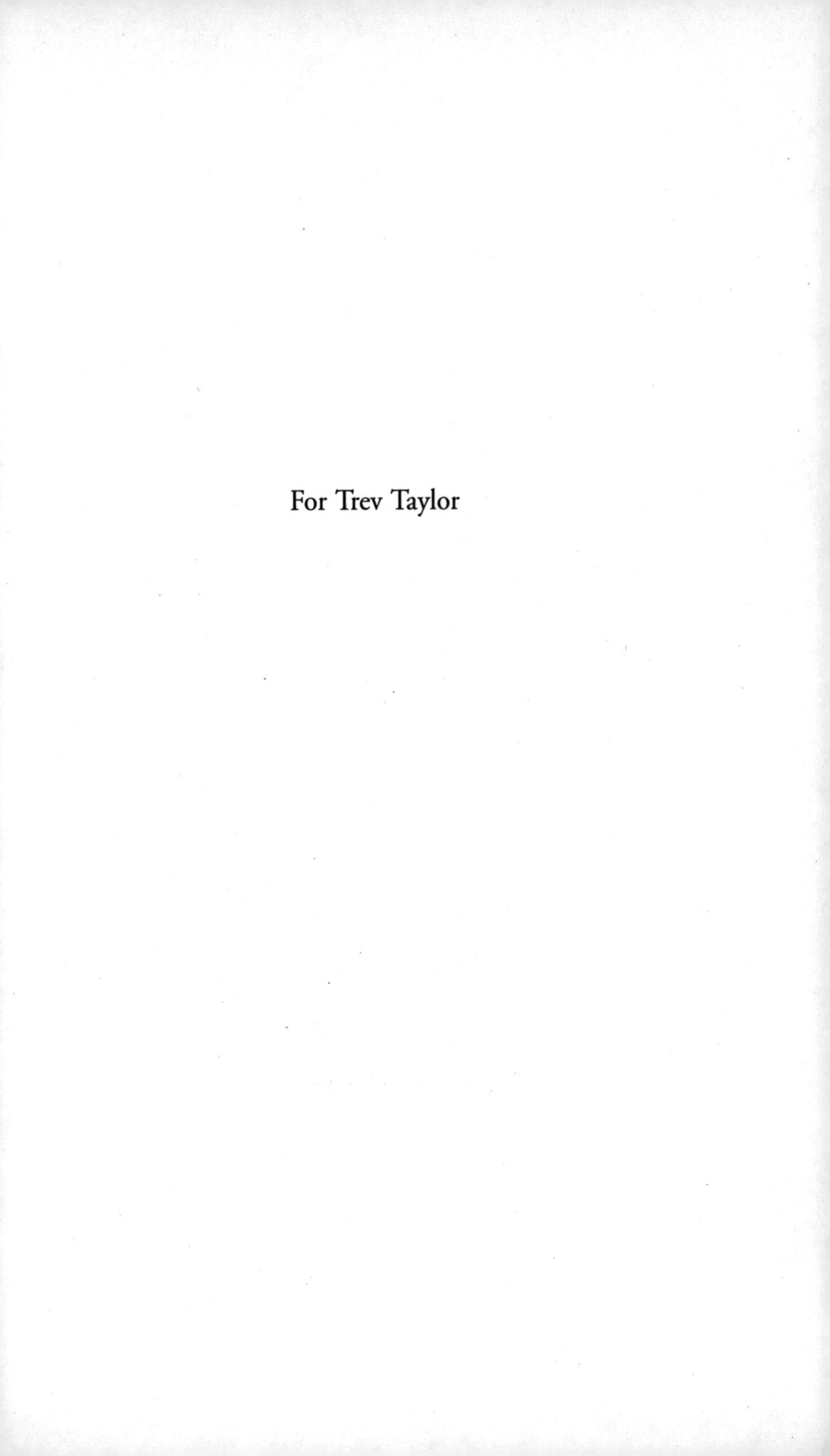

For Trev Taylor

Contents

Hope

1

AS THE AMBULANCE blares towards the Infirmary, I try to look as out-of-it as seems necessary. Can a hundred paracetamol kill you? That's what I told them so they wouldn't make me vomit. The driver tells me not to worry, he's only put the siren on to emotionally blackmail his way through the traffic. They can't pump your stomach with paracetamol, can they? When Julian swallowed them that time, all the blood vessels burst on his face and his tongue went black. Or maybe that was the Cabernet Sauvignon.

The wee lassie that attached me to the monitor looks about twelve. She looked pissed-off when my vital signs showed up normal. I know how to read them having watched Dad slowly die on one. She and her even tinier mate have just carried me from the middle of Saughton Park to the main road. I called 999 from the phone box outside Davie's, then staggered over there.

When we get up to the hospital, I wait until they're busying themselves with the ramp and stretcher before pulling free of the monitor and leaping out into the glow of A & E. As I hit the ground running, I'm halfway across Lauriston Place before they register what's happened. The driver is a fast-moving blur behind me as I sprint into Forrest Road. By the time I get to Desiree's flat on George IV Bridge he's obviously re-read his job description and given up. I have no complaints about the NHS. I've always found it very hospitable.

Desiree's out for the count by the time I arrive, having just received a cassette stuffed with supergrass from Eartha in Laos. A rather misguided children's charity gave Eartha a grant to go there, bugger street kids and post marijuana to his pals for six months. It makes you realise what Comic Relief is really about. I'm going to send them a proposal. Get out of here. Go somewhere hot.

I knock back half a glass of red wine and skin-up before bothering to look up and see who's here. There's always a full complement of people in this room. Some come once, can't handle the slagging fags and never return. Others visit weekly or every few days. Some never seem to leave. Desiree and Eartha usually hold court but in their absence it is rather like a chat show without a host. Splinter groups have been established. They are all probably bitching fiercely about one another. Noticing a woman in her sixties sitting with the pigeon sisters, I wonder if she's our David Dimbleby for the evening.

I slowly start to take in everybody else although I know it's fruitless. There's never any talent here. I've had my cock sucked by a couple of them but only ever through blind drunkenness or unbridled desperation.

Jason squeezes my shoulder and hands me a copy of some treacherously stapled literary mag from the North East. He wants me to look at a poem he has in it and watches my reaction as I read. It is a self-obsessed navel contemplation and as predictably shit as the rest of his stuff. Jason's high opinion of himself really makes me cringe. If there's one thing I hate it's those poor-me-tormented-writer types. Handing the magazine back I feign interest nonetheless and ask if he has anything else in the pipeline.

'I wish. Nobody's interested these days if it's not about asylum seekers or talking dogs. Nobody wants real literature any more.'

'Couldn't you stick a few gypsies in to keep the punters happy?'

He stomps away, feigning offence.

As I spark up the joint, I turn my attention back to the pigeon sisters. Coo is in the midst of an astronomical phase and has been boring the tits off us all for weeks with his black holes and supernovas. Doo has started going to saunas again to illustrate his disquiet. As Coo rambles on about Stephen Hawking's universe, Doo keeps trying to get the conversation down to his level.

'Honestly though, if they have the technology to leapfrog

galaxies surely they could get a better voice for the poor guy.'

The old woman chortles.

'. . . don't you think though, a nice wee Sean Connery or something? Intershtellar coshmanaughtsh. Much more believable.'

Coo is blushing and flustered.

'Oh, you're such an ignorant prick. Your brain's the size of a sixteenth. There's no room for anything new in there,' he says, banging his temple for emphasis. Clattering his chair dramatically, he proffers his back to Doo and attention to the old woman.

'I've never met him before tonight, honestly. Intelligent conversation, please, before I lose all faith in humanity. What are your thoughts on cosmology and the search for dark matter, pray tell?'

The old woman winks at Doo and smiles.

'I'm awfully sorry dear. I watched a couple of documentaries about that chap, but the only thing that really struck me was that so many eminent scientists have subscriptions to *Penthouse*.'

The comment seems to focus everyone's attention on her.

Shirley drapes an arm around me. I hadn't even noticed he was here.

'Speaking of which, Dionne, I'd like you to meet Hope, my auntie. She's been festering away in her huge New Town penthouse since my uncle died. I thought we could do with having someone old and wise round for a change.'

'Hey, less of the wise,' she smirks, raising her glass to me. 'Dionne, is that your real name?'

I can't even remember why or how we ended up addressing each other in such ridiculous ways and suddenly realise how sad it is.

'Martin . . . Martin Bell as it happens.'

'Now he IS an alien,' Doo butts in. Hope blanks him.

'Then I'll call you Martin if you don't mind. These Las Vegas names are all very well but I prefer Hope to Despair.'

'Absolutely.'

Numerous joints circle the table. When Hope is passed one she takes a long draw then blows a smoke ring. She's cool. Not as old as I thought at first, maybe just late fifties, with a Marianne Faithfull sort of clumsy elegance. Intrigued, I pick up my drink and go over.

No sooner have I sat down than Shirley has his big arse squeezed on the back of my chair and whispers unsubtly in my ear, 'Auntie's climbing the walls in that huge flat. See if she fancies a lodger. You must get out that smelly place you're in.'

I push him away awkwardly as Hope frowns and shakes her head.

'Honestly, Angus, I'm not senile, you know? I do still have control over my power of speech. I've no doubt Martin does too.'

The room erupts in laughter. Angus! He told us his real name was Andrew. No wonder he makes us call him Shirley. We try and out-do each other with crap Angus/sheep-shagger jokes until I notice Hope's eyes starting to glaze over and don't want to seem as arse-ish as the rest of them.

'Come on girls, it's like the bloody Gang Show in here. Anyone would think we were smoking real blow.'

The door goes. It's a couple of guys Shirley knows from the Traverse, very fuckable but straight, I've already asked. In line with flat decorum they immediately uncork a bottle of Jacob's Crack and start skinning-up. The effect the youngest guest has on the assembled queens is rather like that of a discarded fish supper on seagulls. I regale Hope with my observation.

'And he thinks I don't get out much!'

It's nice to have someone look me in the eye when they talk to me without reading something into it for a change.

'I didn't even know Shirl . . . Angus had an auntie, or a family for that matter. I just assumed someone had found him in a cabbage patch in London Road in the mid-eighties and handed him in at the Laughing Duck.'

Hope pulls a face.

'We don't really have a family as such. First and second generation black sheep, far too garish for beige people like them.' She gestures to Shirley. 'His father's a church elder, you know, not that the implication of that is what it used to be.'

Replenishing my drink from one of the army of bottles, I offer her some. Fumbling in a carpetbag by her side she produces a half bottle of Ten-Year-Old Macallan's and pours herself a navvy's measure. Shirley sidles through from the kitchen, topping up Hope's glass with hot water, blood orange juice, a spoonful of Tate and Lyle and a stir.

Hope gives him a smile of appreciation, takes a little sip and hugs herself.

'It was my only precondition of coming here tonight. I bring my own bottle though or he tries to palm me off with that revolting Grouse nonsense. Even with their Sunday clothes on I can still tell one from the other.'

'So is that your standard tipple?' I ask her, amused at her extravagance.

'Only when there's someone else to do it for me, or if I know I'm really going to be hitting the sauce. It dehydrates and rehydrates me simultaneously. I never get a bad head, just a good night's sleep.'

I'm completely sold on hot toddies and begin wolfing down the wine, briefly scanning the girls as I swallow. Coo seems to be having most success with the Traverse dream-boat. The rest sulk round them, having one of their little joint-rolling conferences. I don't think I've ever met any of them when they've been straight. Mind you, I'm hardly one to talk. I'm only ever straight at work. Usually! Turning back to Hope I take a long sniff of her drink and go mmmmm.

'Finish that red muck and have one if you wish. Don't let the rest of them near it though or I'll end up on the red muck too.'

I'm flattered that she seems to have singled me out like this and feel a need to disassociate myself from the rest of them. They suddenly seem so childish, superficial.

'So you're having some accommodation trouble I gather?'

Not wanting to sound like a dosser after Shirley's 'smelly place' comment I play it down.

'I'd like a bigger place but they all want a deposit and a month's rent in advance and I resent handing £1200 over to some horrid little Jew before I even spend a night there.'

Oh shit, the anti-Semitic lapse was maybe a bit much. Hope is smiling and seems to have appreciated it though.

'Indeed.'

'Besides, I spend so much time at work I never have time to look at anywhere.'

'What's your line of work?'

God, how embarrassing.

'I manage a bookshop near Stockbridge. Not really what I intended to do with my MA in Fine Arts but you just can't get funding these days.' Does it sound like I'm hustling her? Fuck, I'm just being honest.

'Surely the Arts Council could help you out? What about a Creative Scotland Award?'

'Erm . . . oh yes. I suppose I could try that.' Shit, shit,

shit. I got them to send me a form out to apply last year but I couldn't be arsed to fill it in. She'll think I don't know what I'm talking about now.

Supping her toddie, she glares at me as if she's trying to suss me out. Just as I convince myself she's realised what a twat I am however, she says very matter of factly, 'There's bags of room in my flat. I'm not out of my mind with loneliness as Angus seems to think but you're welcome to stay while you look for somewhere. It's Northumberland Street.'

Northumberland Street! Isn't it that gorgeous Georgian street that all the queens stay in? I'm instantly fantasising about leaving my shithole in Haymarket behind, along with two months' unpaid rent, a kicked-in wardrobe and some extremely dodgy downloads on the flat computer's internet history. I knew there must be a reason I pulled the ambulance stunt to get up here tonight. You never see cabs in Whitson. Nobody can afford them. God, I'm sitting gouching without having responded to Hope's offer.

'Seriously, you wouldn't mind?'

She laughs as if I'm joking. 'What's to mind? You're not a sociopath are you? Angus can vouch for you, can't you Angus?'

Shirley tries to focus his attention away from Traverse-boy. Jesus, don't they get bored being so lecherously queeny all the time? He points at the blood orange carton, not understanding.

'No dear, I'm just wondering if Martin here would be likely to run off with the family silver.'

'I'd let him. Silver's just so passé. Make not bad ashtrays I suppose.'

Jesus, do people really have family silver? I'll be lucky to get a sixteen-piece catalogue special with two chipped saucers and a plate missing when mum pegs out.

Angus gives me the thumbs up regardless and immediately turns his attention back to Traverse-boy who I've decided looks like a young Christopher Walken.

Hope grabs my hand and shakes it till I hear the bones crack.

'See how we get on anyway. Better than throwing money at a horrid little Jew. I've known a few myself.'

I shake back enthusiastically, consciously more firmly than my usual flaccid-penis-in-the-palm thing.

'That's great, honestly, great.'

People are so stupid. They trust implicitly anyone who shows the slightest interest in them. It's loneliness I suppose. Other people can't seem to be comfortable with their own company the way I can, pathetic really. I can make myself like Hope though. I can make myself like anyone.

2

The following day, I go for a few swifties in the New Town after work for my nerves then make my way down to Northumberland Street, to see the flat. As I try to work out the house numbers, I see Hope struggling towards me, two Thresher bags clanking from each arm.

'I thought I should rejuvenate my drinks cabinet if I'm going to have company. Please don't say you're a whisky puritan like myself, I've rather splashed out on lesser things.'

As I wrestle a couple of bags off her, she begins making her way up the steps to one of the houses. It's like a fucking foreign embassy. Then we're on the way up this plush and seemingly endless stair. For a second I think she owns the whole thing. Fuck, these New Town places are only three floors but they seem infinitely higher than normal stairs. By the time we finally reach the top landing, I'm knackered. Hope smiles at my wheezing, looking decidedly unexerted.

'I only keep this place on for the exercise. It's either that or starving myself. I can't abide overweight people.'

The front door opens onto a very long, polished-floored hall. Old film posters are pasted to the walls like they used to be outside cinema two at the Filmhouse. I wonder who stole whose idea. Some of them would be worth a fortune. *The Wizard of Oz* looks like an original, *Lolita, The Servant, The Sweet Smell of Success* – they all look old. Pasted to the bloody walls though, worthless.

'This is absolutely fab. Did you do it yourself?' I ask her, gesturing to a poster for the original *Desperate Hours.* God, Bogie was such a man.

'Good God, no. I don't have the patience. They were

my husband's babies. Completely movie-mad he was. We saw a lot of them together. They remind me of him, in a good way.'

All over the ceiling as well. God, it's so cool. I'm trying to see how many I recognise as she leads me to this enormous kitchen. In the centre is a huge, cast-iron cooking range, overhung by dozens of stainless steel utensils. Honestly, every cooking implement (and some that look like they came out of Guantánamo Bay) you could ever dream of. At the top of the room, by the window, is a massive china sink, like the kind you used to get in art classes and a gorgeous chunky oak breakfast table. It's like a bloody hotel kitchen. I think of the windowless boxroom in my current flat with ochre grease a centimetre deep on the walls. The walls in here are a fresh-looking Habitat green with a stunning abstract-print linoleum floor. Opening the vast fridge door, Hope begins transferring bottles from her bags.

'What's your poison? Wine, beer, champagne? There's spirits in the other room if you'd prefer.'

'Anything, I don't mind.'

Hope extracts the Moët with a flourish.

'How about this to whet our whistles? Carry it round with us as I show you the place.'

Popping it open she hands me a glass with a bowl the size of a grapefruit and pours us both one.

'To you and your kindness.'

She pulls a face and switches off the kitchen light.

'Spare me the sentiment, dear, please, it lulls one into a terribly false sense of security.'

First on the right is this enormous bedroom – big brass double bed, polished floors with a couple of extremely expensive-looking rugs, ornate lead fireplace, with a view right down towards Stockbridge and into the houses of all these rich, lucky bastards. A lovely mahogany wardrobe and chest of drawers; massive old pirate's chest. This must be Hope's room, absolutely exquisite.

'What do you think then? Will it do until you find somewhere else? Don't worry about money. Cook me the odd spaghetti carbonara if you must.'

I'm utterly aghast, already imagining the reactions of the people I'm going to invite here, the ones who try to make me feel inadequate because I don't have my own place. Fuck them and their mortgages.

Hope seems so keen for me to stay, and for free. There will most definitely be a catch but I'm damned if I'm going to worry about that before it makes itself apparent. Could I finally be getting a break?

There are another three bedrooms, all immaculate, like mine, and Hope's, which is packed to the gunnels with books, antiques and boxes looking for a home. You can barely make out her bed amidst the intense camouflage of clutter. Our rooms are at opposite ends of the hall, however it is hers, rather than my own which is conveniently next to the main door. We have a bathroom each, both with gloriously theatrical dressing-room bulbs round the mirrors, perfect for blackheads. It's like bloody Malmaison.

Eventually we retire to the living room, which is so wonderfully chilled-out it's unreal. Again, big, chunky armchairs with ethnic-looking throws over them, massive fireplace, antiques absolutely everywhere, loads of plants.

Hope puts the Moët on the table in front of the fire, switches on an art deco lamp in the corner of the room and tells me to make myself at home. I already am – totally.

We seem to become embroiled in this intense conversation as soon as we sit down. There's none of that ridiculous small talk that Edinburgh people usually use to keep people at a distance till they've decided what to dislike about them. Hope appears to have angles on everything that I'd never even contemplated before and seems able to make any topic interesting. She sells all these wild concepts to me and is encouraging enough to make me think up a few of my own. It's so refreshing. The Scots used to be renowned for their love of a good argument. Now they just bottle it up and go daft. As we finish off the champagne, having smoked a few joints, I start going on about the Holocaust.

'It was more like a revolution if you ask me. Honestly, if there was a major revolution in Britain tomorrow the targets would be the same. All these wee enclosed, self-perpetuating groups of wealthy people – the Jews, the black market,

Freemasons, homosexuals, the aristocracy. You know? They're all we're-all-right-Jack types?'

Whilst I realise I shouldn't really be advocating the gassing of gays I feel like I've suddenly understood what it was actually all about. Like I've just realised how we colonise things – bars, professions, streets, councils – and can be protesting for the right to be accepted one minute and watching someone's grandad take a dump through a hole in a wall the next. I don't want to be gay, I never have. I hate gays and that contempt they have for everyone else. I see it in myself and I hate that too.

In the midst of regaling Hope with my new homophobic philosophy I start to panic that I'm going too far or that I'm getting a bit anything-you-can-think-I-can-think-sicker. I'm pleased with the bit about recognising it in myself though. It makes me seem quite sorted I think. Hope refills our glasses with two huge measures of a seemingly precious bottle of Glencoe though, so she must have appreciated it.

'Oh, I'm a great one for extremes myself, my dear. The middle ground has always bored me silly. Someone once said I should set up a fascio-communist alliance. My politics sort of dangles somewhere along the Bering Straits.'

Although her comment is intended to put me at ease, it unnerves me and I begin to worry about her being more intelligent than me, thinking I'm an arse. Why am I having this sudden downer when I had coke-like confidence a minute ago? To overcome my negative thoughts I study the stack of

CDs by the fireplace, mainly classical, bloody boxed sets – Mozart complete piano sonatas, the whole *Ring*, loads of Bach and baroque stuff which I love, musicals, hundreds of film soundtracks.

Hope tells me to put something on and I start to panic again as I'm certain I'll pick the one she hates, the one she's ashamed of. I'm taking too long so I plump for Debussy and start going on about him dying of fright when he heard the noises of battle coming towards him. Then I realise I'm taking the word of a music teacher, fifteen years ago, who probably made it up in a fruitless attempt to make the pupils more interested. Change the subject, quick!

'I've not noticed a television in the flat. Are you a non-believer?'

'Can't stand it. The real opium of the masses. I can't tell you how many good friends I've seen wither to death in front of the box. It's worse than cancer.'

Oh well, there goes *Newsnight Review* and *Big Brother*.

'It can be terribly manipulative, I suppose.'

'I'll say. Wasn't it originally supposed to be educational and impartial. Bloody propaganda! If I want to learn about something I'll go to a library and make up my own mind, thank you.'

'Not get your opinions prescribed to you by multi-nationals,' I manage to slur out, replenishing my confidence somewhat.

'Precisely!' and she clinks her glass against mine.

My sense of wellbeing gathers momentum again as we begin joking about the things that make life worth living. It's amazing how many queer wee things we have in common – Bob Fosse musicals; DH Lawrence; really fishy seafood; the cult of Terry Wogan (and she was snooty about TV?); the Q&A in the Saturday *Guardian* being the best bit; sitting amongst cows and the smells of the London Underground; tar; carbolic soap; baked potato shops; and these little white bits you cough up sometimes. Jesus, and I thought I was the only one.

Then we start on our dislikes. We resolutely agree on mobile phones; cars; media witchhunts; people who tell you to cheer up just because you're not grinning inanely; the tragedy of bad smells during beautiful moments; snoring; any form of audible breathing; mothers who don't need to work but do (hi mum!); the Middle East (both sides); and people who break wind in public.

Then Hope doesn't respond to my 'women who have abortions because they want a life' (hi again, mum, I didn't want a brother anyway). If that doesn't make me paranoid enough, she then comes out with 'confidence tricksters' and 'people who rip-off the Health Service' in quick succession.

I don't know how long I sit with a stupid look on my face before managing a measly, 'people who go on about their sun tans' (Hope and myself are both peely-wally and interesting) and the fact that the *Daily Record* is the biggest-selling newspaper in Scotland. I realise how crap they are as soon as I've said them but it's too late now anyway. These little rushes of unpleasantness are starting to get the better of me and I want to go. She can't see me puking in the toilet before I even move in.

Wolfing down the remainder of my whisky, and stifling a subsequent boak, I say I'll have to go, work in the morning, all that shit. Hope welcomes me to stay the night but I want back to my moisturiser and my Ribena and just that pile of rubbish I call home. Once I've moved it here, this will be home. That is the nature of rubbish.

As I won't be able to flit for a couple of days (the landlord's always snooping around for the rent on Wednesdays and Thursdays) I give her my work number in case she changes her mind. I'm only thinking about the good bits by the time I get in the taxi. Northumberland Street, you cunt!

3

I busy myself for the next couple of nights hassling the local grocers for cardboard boxes and savagely disposing of a lot of my belongings in the name of a lighter-travelling existence. Having to work until six both nights doesn't help. I have loads of annual leave to take but it's not cost effective. Besides, I'm saving it up for a big blow-out, maybe a cruise.

Generally, the majority of my working days are spent constructively anyway, i.e. not working. Hope and I have a few long phone calls at my boss's expense. It's good to have someone intelligent to talk to for a change.

I'm lucky if I get three hours' sleep on the Thursday, my last night in Shitsville, as I'm thinking about that gorgeous flat and the people I'm going to show it to and potentially good times with Hope. Life does smile on me sometimes. I must take advantage of it this time.

Leaving for work the next morning for the last time is glorious. At the side of the bulging wheelie bin, my excess baggage lies strewn for the binmen along Haymarket Terrace, like the staff of Number Ten bidding farewell to an outgoing Prime Minister. Though I leave ten minutes after I should have opened up I take my time to gaze at the shit-stained road for hopefully the second last time. Who buys second-hand books at ten in the morning anyway? I've been running the shop on my own since my boss retired three months ago. He just pays the bills now.

Cutting down Palmerston Place I walk along the Water of Leith. The smell of rotting vegetation is as refreshing to me as sea air. As I pass under the Dean Bridge, I recall a fuck I had down here with an old wino in my early teens. He could only summon a semi, but it was huge. I had sparse pubes at the time, which really drove him wild, but he stank of rotting liver.

An old bloke walks past with his dog, jolting me out of my thoughts with a ridiculous, 'Cheer up, it's not the end of the world.' Christ, we were just talking about that the other night. People do actually still say it. I give the old tosser a smile anyway. He has a complexion like an uncooked beef sausage.

It's 10.25 by the time I get to the shop. In the unlikely event that Callum the owner's phoned to check I'm in on time, I'll just say I forgot to switch the answering machine off. Another plus of not having a mobile phone. No messages though, no calls and no customers for most of the morning. Leisurely speeding myself up with black coffee, I listen to Classic FM and throw myself into the *Scotsman* crossword. Sometimes I really like routine.

A Goth-looking lassie comes in about 11.15 and tries to sell me a bag of John Mortimer. How is there so much fucking John Mortimer, John Galsworthy and Raymond Chandler in the world? I think they breed with each other on the shelves at Barnardo's. Having regaled the lassie with my observation, she looks suitably embarrassed, then slopes back to Transylvania.

Occasionally in this shop I'll get offered a little gem but generally it's scruffy twenty-somethings who sell me course books, get used to the extra money then bring in their film books, then the Penguin Classics till eventually it's the spanking new never-read book club editions and they come in with tears in their eyes. I take books off these student bastards I know I can sell for a couple of hundred pounds, get them to sign for enough money for a sixteenth, then stick a two or three in front of the £7.50 when they leave – everybody's happy! Stewart only pays me £120 a week, after tax. I'll be saving £45 a week on the flat now so that can go straight in my Instant Access Savings Account. The rest of my money usually gets tied up in debts I haven't been able to dump and my blow. For entertainment I usually aim to fiddle about £50 a day which is piss easy via a subtle combination of over-charging, under-ringing, altering figures and private sales. The shop only takes about £150 a day but Callum hasn't checked the accounts in ages. The cancer will finish him off in a few months anyway. He's not going to waste his time book-keeping now.

By closing-up time I'm pretty excited about the move but starting to feel a bit edgy about cohabiting with a woman I've only known for three days who's older than my mother. I don't want to end up like some Tennessee Williams toy boy. Do women her age still want sex? Surely not. Is it obvious enough that I'm gay? She is all right though, I'm sure. I know I was pissed but we've been fine on the phone since and we have a laugh together. Besides, I read somewhere that mothers are supposed to be the new fashion accessory.

4

One taxi journey is enough to transfer the few worldly belongings I haven't binned to my new street. The three boxes of junk and expandable case full of clothes take only two treks up and down the stairs. A previous entourage of books and records were sold long ago in less flush days. My current occupation is a symptom of this.

Hope flutters around as I feather my new nest with my minimalist belongings, trilling along to a Kurt Weill CD. Adding a few postcards and random drapings of white muslin, I roll a joint. Unwinding with the first few puffs I take it through to Hope with a bottle of Bowmore I got her on the way back from work.

'For me, darling? How sweet.'

'Just to say thanks, you know, for letting me stay. I'll find my own place as soon as I can.'

'If you'd rather be on your own, that's fine. You're welcome here though, no rush. No more presents though, ok?'

She hands me back the spliff as I follow her through to the living room. I'm expecting a whisky but she puts the Bowmore in a cupboard and squeezes past me into the hall again.

'I'm going to be away for the night. You don't mind, do you? You won't be scared?'

'Erm, no, that's fine,' I stammer, slightly taken aback. 'Going anywhere exotic?'

She slings a shawl dramatically around her shoulders and grimaces at me.

'Not exactly, well not unless your idea of exotica is line dancing in Loanhead.'

I laugh too forcefully.

'Oh I know, dear. I went there with some friends about three months ago though and I'm completely hooked. Pathetic, isn't it. Anyway, it's one of the few places I can go and still feel faintly glamorous.'

Biting back a mumble of patronising clichés about being good for her age, I settle for a simple, 'I know the feeling.'

Then the front door's open and she's rushing out excitedly.

'Try to enjoy yourself and if you do burn the house down, make sure it looks like an accident – insurance, you know? I should be back tomorrow evening sometime. Be a good boy,' and she pats my cheek and launches down the stairs.

I feel quite stunned for some reason as I wave over the bannister at her. As she gets to the bottom she shouts up, 'I go to the occasional rave as well,' then I hear the stair door slam. It's more than I do.

Going back into the flat I stand and stare along the huge empty hall. My huge empty hall. Fuck two years of celibacy. I'm bringing a man back here tonight.

5

Time seems to pass so quickly as you get older. It seems as if the South Bank Show's on every night of the week. My system never gets time to recover between drinking bouts. What the hell, it's predominantly wine I drink, which is good for you anyway. Drinking is preferable to eating. The choice between two bottles of claret or a meal is a simple one. Eating's time consuming and makes you look so bloody bad. I'm lucky if I have one proper meal a week but I still look fat. I can feel my ribs through my jumper but I'm terribly podgy about the abdomen.

Going to my enormous, gorgeous room, I stick Garbage on, uncork the bottle of red wine I bought myself and roll a massive spliff. Striding about, knocking back the drink, I look at the view down to Dublin Street and across towards Stockbridge, into the lives of all these rich fuckers and I think here I come, you bastards, here I fucking come.

I sit down on the bed and begin fantasising about all the different people I'm going to bring back here. What their reactions will be. Then I have a prolonged dwam about slapping this little chicken I have my eye on about the place and almost get a hard-on. When I come to, it's 9.45, and the wine's nearly finished. Two and a half hours have vanished. This happens a lot these days. I go into myself and can't find the way out.

Forcing myself under the shower, it feels fantastic after the dirty, fibreglass tub I've been subjected to for the past three years. Feeling suitably invigorated I study my nakedness in the bathroom's full-length mirror. Jesus, my belly gets bigger every time I look at it. Maybe I should shave my pubes again. It might help me feel hornier.

Despite my liberating flit from Haymarket I feel

strangely drawn to my old local. Faggots have been slowly streaming into it over the past few years and it's now more or less a gay bar but with the odd hairy arsed workman. The other guys remain unconvinced and refuse to go there with me.

I want someone with me tonight though, an accomplice, someone to do all the talking while I stalk my prey. Jesus, listen to me. Who am I kidding? I'm beginning to think I'm completely unshaggable. Some speed might help, but it always makes me psychotic and I feel like topping myself for about a week afterwards. It's just the physical act of snorting it I like. It goes pear-shaped after that.

Once I'm outside and fully conscious of where I am, I see sense about my Haymarket idea, and allow my feet to drag me easterly, to the Phoenix. As I swing into a room full of vodka-breathed people it seems not a bad decision. I always see someone I know in here, I think, a second before seeing Simon, a guy I know from Sainsbury's Central who's usually good for a bit of toot. Standing at the bar with him I begin to think my life is either charmed or I am psychic.

Simon gets me a double Black Label Smirnoff and Diet Coke. It's so cheap in here it's untrue. We go up the steps, sit looking down on the bar and I painlessly score a gram off him. There is a guy at the juke box with his dog, acned ugly bastard but wearing football shorts which I love. There's something about that flimsy layer of fibre between me and a cock. My ultimate fantasy is to be at a football match, standing beside some wee kids and their dad, someone like Duncan Ferguson getting tripped-up in front of us and his three-piece falling out the bottom of his shorts. I saw a photo of that very phenomenon in a magazine a few years ago but I thought of it first. I made Duncan's balls fall out.

Simon starts telling me about his friend in the Western with pneumonia, being on his last legs. The last time I saw the guy was about two months ago in the New Town. He had on a cropped t-shirt to show off his suspicious sarcomas. He works for an AIDS charity as well. Mind you, everyone I know that works for an AIDS charity is HIV positive. It doesn't do much to reinforce my faith in safe sex.

Was I sitting gouching when he was telling me about his pal dying? Oh God, he's talking about Joy Division now. Simon always seems to bring every conversation round to bloody Joy Division or bands he thinks are trying to sound like Joy Division. The singer died about 20 years ago didn't he? They were crap anyway.

'Did I tell you about the time I saw them support the Buzzcocks at the Odeon?'

'I think you have, yeah, you definitely have.'

About a thousand times. I start checking out the bar for possible means of escape from misery-guts as there's no way I'm spending my night talking about John Peel and the cowie. The guy in the football shorts gives me a thin smile as I catch his eye. There's something really horny about ugly guys. They look like they're game for anything, and they're usually so grateful you're taking them on they go mad for it. I've seen him before a few times but I can't remember where.

I tell Simon I'm going to the cigarette machine and get up. The guy is still clocking me, blatantly, I love that. Pretending to put money in the machine, I push the button for Silk Cut. It rumbles, I slap it and walk back up to the table.

'They've run out, I'm just going over to the chippie.'

Simon has started chatting to a guy with fluorescent orange hair and merely nods in acknowledgement without looking round.

Walking out the pub I sense the guy with the shorts following me. My legs go a bit shaky, it's so fucking long since I've done anything like this. He comes out behind me, just like I expect him to. Joe Orton was right. I don't know how you know, you just do. This surge of bravado just comes from nowhere. When I pretend to go back into the pub he blocks my way, grinning.

'You don't really want to go back in there, do you?'

'What would you suggest like?'

He shrugs his shoulders and we both walk back towards my new pad with his mutt. The last two days have had a dream-like simplicity about them.

6

His snoring wakes me in the middle of the night. I'm horrified to find him beside me and even more horrified to find his smelly dog squeezed in between us. How could a bottle of red wine and a vodka be so kind on the features of someone so grotesque? The snoring makes him doubly unappealing. I stare at him for a minute with an uneasy mix of anger and morbid fascination till the sound of his honking drives me out of the room. My rage is then propounded by a recollection of me not being able to get a proper hard-on when he tried to suck me off. I want him out of here, I wish he was dead. Did he say he was from Haymarket? That's where I've seen him before. Thank fuck I'm away from there now.

Stomping through to the living room, I attempt to roll a joint but my hands are shaking because I'm so annoyed. Just be assertive, I tell myself. Striding back through to the bedroom, I stand beside the bed looking down at him.

'Hey, hey pal. Wake up.'

He just lies snoring. I give him a gentle shake. 'Hey, come on, you'll have to go.' Still no response so I shake him more firmly. Surely that should have woken him up. Perhaps he's pretending to be asleep. I jostle him until he rolls onto his back. Still the awful noise continues. The anger is pumping adrenaline through my body. Lifting the quilt up, I grab his feet and pull him off the bed. As he thuds onto the floor his head cracks on the floorboards. Shit, I panic but the pain wakes him and he fumbles blindly for the duvet, wondering what's going on.

'I'm sorry but I'd rather you went home. Nothing personal you know. I just need some time on my own.'

He seems confused but ok about it all and starts stumbling into his ridiculous outfit again. Not knowing what to say, I go back through to my joint as the decisive action has curtailed my trembling. After a couple of minutes he comes through to say goodbye.

As I open the front door, I allow him to kiss me, just so he'll go away.

'Do you live here now then?'

Though I don't want him to know I do, the pose is almost irresistible. Compromising I give him a what-do-you-think shrug.

'Probably bump into you again sometime,' I say as I shut the door, knowing that life can sometimes be that cruel. Dammit, and the Phoenix is so convenient now.

Stripping the covers off my bed I stuff them in the washing machine. Remembering the joint, I take it through to my bedroom and start rummaging through one of my unpacked boxes of stuff. Why have I let that bastard get to me? I'm on a real downer now because I've sacrificed two years of celibacy for someone so inconsequential.

Hyper-alert through rage and remnants of the speed, I thumb through photos of myself as a teenager and think what a fat geek I was. I find a ticket for BB King at the Playhouse from years ago and remember my hot date that night with a computer salesman I met in a toilet, who said he was going to take me away from it all. We snogged in the middle row. He told me I made him feel like James Dean. That was the last time I saw him. I hate BB King. My 1992 diary keeps coming to the top of the pile of junk but I'm trying to ignore it as diary-reading makes me feel like such an old fag. Perhaps one random page won't hurt.

Monday 7 May 1992

Mum lost her job. Wept a lot. Felt panicky and angry all day.

Tuesday 8 May 1992

Felt depressed in the morning but was unemotional by bedtime.

Wednesday 9 May 1992

Felt neither here nor there in morning. Threw a wobbly in a restaurant. Unemotional for the rest of the day.

Thursday 10 May 1992

Watched *Taxi Driver*. Felt mildly paranoid. Felt OK at night.

Friday 11 May 1992

Felt fine all day. Couldn't sleep.

Saturday 12 May 1992

Felt bad when I woke up. Didn't get Napier job. Thought when I was happy it was perhaps only mania. Felt better at night but couldn't sleep.

Jesus, have I always been such a sad bastard? I go back to bed but can hardly think for thinking about it.

7

Waking up in my new home is rather disorientating and my first thought is that I must have copped with some old pouve or other. Once I've opened the shutters (yes, proper shutters, it's like fucking Paris), got Maria Callas blaring and christened my new toilet it feels significantly more homely. I devote most of the morning to swallowing strong black coffee (proper stuff, natch), smoking joints and nosing round the flat. Hope has some amazing clothes – as if Lena Martell, Quentin Crisp and the cast of a blaxploitation movie maybe shared a wardrobe at some point. Everything smells of her, in a good way.

Rummaging through her drawers, I'm intrigued to find out what kind of knickers she might wear. The bland, pastel-shaded Marks and Spencer briefs sort of disappoint me but are at least better than the shoulder-length passion-killers mum wears.

Noticing a *Miller's Antiques Guide* in the tightly crammed bookcase I wrench it out and begin thumbing through it. Maybe I can identify some of the things she has stashed in here. It's tiresome at first having to negotiate the lopsided weight of the flimsy pages. As I squint at the tiny print of the index and slowly begin to find things though, I start to really get into it. Hours pass as I study dishes, ornaments, sideboards, prints, totting up figures, not with any master plan in mind, just because I'm enjoying teaching myself about it all.

By teatime I'm bored with it and exhausted by my own enthusiasm. Feeling listless and strangely alone I'm back in full-fledged sad bastard mode again in no time at all. When Hope's not back by seven I feel so frustrated I have to go for a lie down. I want to go out somewhere where there's no faggots, just for a change. Drawing a blank on suitable ideas I watch light dancing on the ceiling from the cars outside till I finally hear the door being unlocked. It's half eight. Hope drifts in singing 'Man, I Feel Like a Woman'. Jumping out of bed I rush into the hall to greet her like a dog that's been on its own too long. She does a bit of her line dancing for me and I'm so pleased to see another human being again, it seems good.

'Oh it's trite but I love it. Don't you get like that sometimes?'

She hangs up her cape and I follow her through to the living room.

'No major disasters? No urban insurrection in Dublin Street? My God, this place looks unnervingly pristine, my dear. Was it a wild party or are you a Virgo?'

'Just a Virgo, I'm afraid. I'm very anal about dust.'

She feigns horror.

'I'll try to be liberal about it, darling, but I'm allergic to dust myself. Who am I to make spiders homeless?'

As she floats around the room, animated, I think how full of life she is and how empty of it I am. I think of my own mother – defeated, bowed and living for the bingo. Maybe energy is genetic. Hope tells me she has tickets for a whisky tasting at Waterstone's and asks if I want to go with her. It sounds just about right. Maybe some of her will rub off on me.

8

The tasting is downstairs at the East End Waterstone's. A red-faced wag with a bushy beard describes each malt with such affection and desire that I almost manage to convince myself that I'm not only here for the beer. The really peaty ones are absolutely divine. My first two have me that safe, glowy way. Hope is circulating and seems to know everyone intimately. I've still no idea what her background is or where all the money comes from. It's too soon to ask her outright.

A few of the staff I know through Shirley are buzzing around but I'm in one of my shy moods, so just stand in a growing daze, tripping-out over the whisky. My favourite is Isle of Jura because it smells like poppers and takes me from gloriously glowy to borderline pissed so beautifully. As I lean against one of the tables, a heavily made-up creature of indeterminate gender gestures to two measures at my side and stammers,

'Pleashe . . . away . . . I'm fucking guttered.'

Knowing that two more will probably push me over the edge I sniff both and knock them back. Jesus, whisky makes me feel really straight. It's such a manly drink.

By the time Hope gets round to me, queasiness is making the thought of a joint and an armchair very attractive. Arm-in-arm with the man who gave the talk, she introduces me as her flatmate. Giving my hand a limp, clammy shake he begins quizzing me about what I do, where I come from, what I think of Edinburgh, how I know Hope, which I'm not really up to lying about. The way he launches at me and the intense eye contact suggest he's quite taken by me but he has terrible halitosis and I have to turn my head when he speaks to me. Hope observes with a worryingly conniving look. I'm starting to wish I'd stayed in. Why is it always the ugly blokes who go for me? If once, just once, a little *Death in Venice* chicken would return my glance, but no, it's always those seedy, cruisey types who don't wash their genitals very often. Why can't I force myself to like people? I don't really like anyone, particularly myself.

Hope though, I do like, but I don't want to be here. I always feel like a nonce unless I'm around people who seem less self-assured than myself. Oh God, Hope has just catapulted herself into a circle of luvvies and embraced everyone. The racket of their squawking and the fanfare of own trumpets being blown is grating on me. Now she's wittering away to the trannie person that gave me its drinks, their faces almost touching as they converse. The spectacle upsets me somehow. What am I thinking? Why do I suddenly feel jealous about some old woman? I'm sick of this.

Barging up to Hope I tell her I'm leaving, I don't feel well. Her eyes try to speak to me out of the jumble of sycophants. Standing like a prick for a few minutes, expecting her to come over, she doesn't, so I make for the exit.

Walking out onto Princes Street, I feel like a Christmas puppy in March. The cemetery in Waterloo Place blinks seductively at me but I feel like I don't want that any more. I don't know what I want.

The walk back to the flat does nothing to lift a feeling of growing doom. I can't even be bothered to roll a joint when I get in. Besides, my chest is fucked because the blow at the moment is full of plastic. Home by nine on a Saturday night. It's fucking shocking. Lying fully dressed on the bed I listen to little cracks of noise outside. Am I destined to spend the rest of my life watching car lights on the ceiling? I just want Hope to come home. I'm lonely. I want to know that she likes me. I want to win her over. I'm still sitting waiting at one the next morning. Getting up, I close the shutters, undress, then get back into bed. What a sad bastard.

9

Despite my early night, the blackened windows allow me to block out the world until well after noon the next day. Hope is back as I can hear her singing about the flat. The sound is faintly erotic. It feels like we're lovers who've had a tiff. I worry about myself sometimes. Irritated by my feeling of non-specific mardiness, I force myself out of bed, stretching flamboyantly as I walk over to open the shutters. The streets below are that quiet, restrained Sunday way, as if the houses have all been abandoned. Perhaps I should do some sketches and flog them to the rich bastards that live around here.

Then I notice a figure opposite the flat, just standing against the railings. I look away then back to confirm the signal my eyes are sending to my brain. Jesus, surely not. It's the ugly bloke I brought back the other night, just standing there with that fucking stinky dog. What the fuck is he playing at? What does he want? Hope can't find out about Friday night, she'll think I'm such a scab. Fuck, fuck, fuck! Should I ignore him or go and see what he wants? How long has he been there?

Hurriedly struggling into my black Levi's I look down again. What a fucking weirdo. He's just standing there smoking. The sight of such an eyesore in my lovely new street offends me. Once I've finished dressing I go through to the living room and ask Hope if she needs anything from the shops. She points to a reading room's-worth of newspapers on the coffee table.

'Most of the papers are there, dear. They keep me entertained until at least Wednesday. There's cholesterol in the fridge.'

'I'm just after some fresh air, really,' I blush. God, this is pathetic. How can leading a charmed life be so complicated? I've decided to take the guy for a pint as I don't want us having a barney in the street. We can go round to the New Town. It's usually full of creeps anyway. Christ, what if the bang on the head yesterday morning's turned him into a psycho?

He gives me a huge smile and starts walking towards me before I'm even out the stair. Jesus, I can't even remember his name. Standing stiffly, I allow him to kiss me then push myself out of his embrace and towards the pub.

'I was just trying to work up the nerve to come up and see you.'

Hell, no.

'Look, it's not convenient for you to come round the house. I live with someone. They were away the other night. We'll have a drink,' and I bluster onwards, unable to attempt communication again until I have a pint in front of me. He walks briskly at my side, gibbering away a lot of shite about the New Town, trying to impress me with historical details I couldn't give a toss about. Why am I even allowing this wanker the courtesy of giving him the brush-off face-to-face?

We sit at the back of the pub, me with a pint, he with a bloody Mary. As his arm sneaks round the back of my shoulders, I push him off.

'Look, pal, the other night, like. Is it OK if we just leave it at that? I shouldn't have taken you back, I'm sorry.'

'Did your mother never tell you not to go with strangers when you were little?' he smirks, refusing to take me seriously. Gulping back a third of my pint, I try again.

'Seriously though, you won't come round again, will you?'

Leaning back, he takes a contemplative sip of his vodka.

'Married, are you?'

'No . . . well, sort of . . . it's kind of complicated.'

He suddenly starts raising his voice. Thankfully it's empty up the back where we're sitting.

'Why do arseholes like you make yourselves available if you're not prepared to go all the way? Fuck, I must be some sort of magnet to bastards like you. You think you can just fuck me and forget it, eh?'

Now he's standing up, hands on hips, having a right queeny fit. What a mess.

'Ok, ok, I'm a bastard, I know. So will you keep away?'

Vodka and tomato juice are running down my face, my eyes smarting with Worcester Sauce. Making for the bogs, I hear the pub door being yanked open violently. Fuck! Grabbing a toilet roll from one of the cubicles I feel something slimy on my fingers and notice cum squirted across the tissue. Yelling, 'Bastard!', I kick the cubicle wall in anger and hear a terrified voice inside squealing, 'Fucking hell!'. Heading for the exit, I see the barman surrounded by a little huddle of poofs, cackling away, watching where we'd been sitting on close-circuit TV behind the bar.

'You don't want to go upsetting that one,' someone laughs at me as I leave.

10

I almost expect him to be standing outside when I leave for work the following morning. Still feeling quite unnerved by yesterday's performance, I find myself checking behind me as I cut down through Canonmills. Once I'm inside the safety of the shop I castigate myself for my paranoia. As long as I avoid the Phoenix it'll be fine.

Once I'm settled with my coffee and a fag, I start reflecting on the previous night. Hope's sort of flirting with me, I'm sure she is. She put her feet up on my legs when we were sitting on the settee together. Her heel against my balls gave me a semi. If she noticed she certainly didn't seem to mind. What the fuck is going on there? I have to sort it out.

Every time the shop door goes, I jump. Shirley phones at lunch time to tell me he's coming round for a visit tonight. I find myself feeling strangely envious that he's known Hope all his life. I'm thinking about her a lot – about our conversations and her voice and her strong, intelligent face. It's almost like I miss her. This feeling intensifies as the day progresses, until at three I ring her on the pretence of telling her that her nephew's coming round, knowing they'd made the arrangement prior to him speaking to me.

'I've just got a few chums round for Canasta, they're leaving soon.'

'Erm . . . have you spoken to Angus?'

'Oh yes, round about eight he said. Anyway, must dash. They'll be cheating next door.'

I'm just mumbling, glad to hear her voice.

'OK . . . erm, yes, well, see you later.'

'Martin?'

'Yes?'

'I missed having you around today. It felt strange . . .'

Although I want to tell her I feel the same, I mumble a bit more then tell her I have to go. God! I bang my head off the desk. What an arsehole I am. I'm bewildered by my own emotions.

11

In the evening Hope cooks us up a Mexican sensation with tacos and nachos and lots of gorgeous little side dishes which I force myself to eat some of. We drink tequila slammers and at one point the three of us are lying on the carpet, hysterical. Shirley is singing Ethel Merman numbers to himself, obscured by the table. As I roll onto my side to get up, my eyes meet Hope's and stay there for a few seconds. Despite a terrific urge to kiss her, I feel my face starting to flush and stand up.

'I almost thought you were going to kiss me, there,' she says, half-joking, half-serious. Laughing the comment off as ridiculous, I embroil myself in the rolling of a joint.

Shirley and Hope talk a lot about her husband and I insist she gets some photos out. He is a tall, elegant looking man, chiselled-bone structure, but despite his acute angular look there's a gentle excitement in his eyes. Hope only shows me one wedding photo and shields her face in embarrassment until it's put away. They were married in a registry office in the sixties, which I think is quite cool. Hope is wearing a trouser suit, like a man's pinstripe, tailored and tapered at the waist for a woman. Her hair is short and her face is radiant and full of mischief. It's almost as if someone has cut a photo out of last month's *Cosmo* and pasted it on. Apparently, her family thought she was a lesbian prior to her wedding. The suit, Savile Row, was a stab at them.

'You've no idea how threatened a lot of people were by the sight of a woman in a trouser suit. I still sometimes wear it for a lark.'

I'm sitting staring at her, as I can blame my fixed gaze on the cannabis. I'd really like to paint her in that suit. When I suggest it to her she seems utterly flattered and insists that I allow her to commission me. Unbelievable, getting paid to do what I feel compelled to do anyway.

Before long, Hope is lying on the settee with her feet on my lap again. As I massage her toes and soles, she writhes around beside me.

'You two seem quite taken with each other,' Shirley observes as we become increasingly touchy-feely.

Hope leans forward and kisses my cheek.

'Martin is giving me a new lease of life, not that I was ever as mothballed as you seemed to think. We plan to marry in the Fall.'

'What a riot, having old Dionne here as an uncle. Cool.'

'Watch your tongue lad or you'll feel my slipper on your arse,' I scold unamusingly, but we collapse into drug-induced hysterics nonetheless. I'm having my most relaxed time in ages but I'm also aware that it is getting on for midnight and Shirley is making no signs of leaving. I want to be alone with Hope in this state and see what happens. But then she makes hot toddies for us, and more joints are rolled until, at 1.30, Shirley's eyes start to flicker and he crashes sideways in the armchair. I try shouting over to startle him before he becomes unconscious but he's already started snoring. Hope swallows down the remainder of her toddie, then pulls herself wearily off me.

'I'm going to follow his example. Give me a knock before you go to work, would you, I'm playing golf at ten,' then she blows me a kiss and leaves me with the snoring bastard. The moment's gone now anyway. Perhaps it's for the best. I've probably just got a wee boarding school crush, you know, I shouldn't necessarily act on it. The sound of Shirley's snoring is reminding me of that little runt the other night. My eyes wince in recollection of the sting of Worcester Sauce as I retire.

12

Hope gets up before I leave in the morning and makes me a coffee as I shave. She looks gloriously wrecked. Sometimes I judge people's beauty on how good they'd be to paint. Hope scores highly on this. Shirley has vanished, God knows when. I'm annoyed that he could plausibly have left shortly after we went to bed and I still could have made a move. Made a move, what am I on about? The new day has made me timid again. Perhaps it's better just to keep it all in my head. You can control situations if you keep them cerebral.

The doorbell goes as I'm about to leave. A woman in her thirties stands behind an eruption of white roses. The lump of envy in my throat disperses when she tells me they're for Martin. The name on the envelope stuck to the wrapper confirms this but I still look at her as if she's joking, grab the flowers and in panic shut the door in her face. My immediate instinct is to open it again and apologise, but I'm too agitated. Hope is in the bathroom, thank God. Smuggling the rustling package into my room, I tremblingly tear open the envelope.

'Forgot to say. You sucked my cock beautifully. Rxxx.'

I feel sick, in fact I bring up and swallow a mouthful of coffee. My shoulders become very sore all of a sudden. Fuck

fuck fuck. Tearing the remainder of the envelope from the wrapper, I stuff it, with the card, under my mattress. Grabbing one of my Lucien Freud postcards off the wall, I scrawl, 'Thanks. Last Present, honest!' regretting it immediately but throw it and the flowers on the telephone table regardless and run out the house. White roses are just so gorgeous. If they'd been tacky red they'd have gone straight in the bin.

Running round to Dublin Street, I hail the first taxi I see. I don't want anyone following me to the shop. It's my safe haven.

13

I'm in pieces at work. He'll be standing outside the flat when I get back tonight, I know he will. I've never been violent towards another human being but I've done some serious damage to inanimate objects in my time. Who knows how I'd react under pressure? It feels as if I'm being violated. What right does the ugly creature feel he has to hassle me like this? I'm an attractive guy. As if I'd get involved with that. Would I be letting it get to me as much if Hope wasn't in the equation? The fact is I would. When people try to invade my space and time it really pisses me off. I make my own decisions about if and when I see people and I hate anyone who tries to interfere with that. I'd get the police onto him but I realise I can't really. It would just bring it out in the open even more; besides, they'd piss themselves laughing.

I'm rude to the few customers we have because I'm so stressed out. At one point I put a 'back in 10 minutes' sign on the door and go to the back of the shop for a joint, but this just serves to make me even more tense. Sometimes I think I get no hit from cannabis any more, that I'm completely immune. Having a joint at work always dispels this theory though, as the surroundings really seem to intensify the hit. It also makes time drag something awful.

I'm kinder to the customers after the smoke, and end up nervously raving to them about the books they're buying. About 2.30 a guy comes in with a large cardboard box. He looks like Harold Shipman. Turns out he's flogging these extremely rare, immaculate art books – Lucien Freud, Bacon, Kitaj and one on the Scottish Colourists with actual prints by Cadell in it. Books I had no idea even existed. In Italian, mind you, but the sort of people that buy books like these are all cunnilingual anyway. I can tell that parting with them really pains the guy, something about the CSA being on his back. Business is business though and I tell him that my business is slow and hum and haw in my usual way till he's really desperate. After torturing him like this for a while, I offer thirty quid for the lot and he predictably jumps at it, looking thoroughly sick as he does. I can probably get that for each of them. Entering them in the ledger as indiscriminate 'Art Books (several)' I make sure to leave plenty of space between the pound sign and the thirty. When he leaves I stash an amazing book of Egon Schiele plates in my bag at the back of the shop, make a coffee and settle down to look through the rest of them, feeling infinitely happier. A few hundred pounds for two minutes' ham acting. Now I know how Sean Connery feels.

I've only just started to price them when a woman comes over with a hefty tome on Raeburn that's been collecting dust since I started here. She spots the Colourists book and asks me how much. I've no idea what it's worth. It's a fucking antique – could be hundreds, could be thousands. As it's not even been named in the ledger I hazard a guess at ninety pounds. The woman's face lights up as she pulls twenty pound notes from her purse and I know I've made a huge boo boo. Too late to worry about it now though and it means I've made a cool two hundred today including ten pounds on my first sale this morning. As I put the books in a bag for her, she thanks me profusely. The difference between her joy and the anguish of the guy who sold me them is striking. She's probably his ex-wife and followed him here.

Buoyed by my burgeoning wealth I start thinking about holidays. Maybe Hope and I could go away somewhere together. I've only been out of Britain twice, to Paris, since I got my passport and it runs out in a couple of years. She'd be good, intelligent company to travel abroad with. She could teach me so much. Perhaps I should suggest it anyway, she'd probably insist on financing the whole trip.

About two o'clock a spotty bloke in a donkey jacket

comes in with a holdall and tells me he has a few Williams first editions to sell. I can't believe it, 'Tennessee Williams?' I confirm. He looks at me blankly. 'Naw, Raymond.' I suppose one coup a day is enough.

After that, the shop is dead. Not that I mind, as I've had a good innings and I'm content to just put my feet up for the rest of the afternoon. Making a coffee I engross myself in my Egon Schiele book. The bell above the shop door tinkles and before I even look up, I get the strange sense that I'm not going to like what I see. First it's the horrible fucking dog, then the creep, smiling, coming towards me.

'Any nice surprises with the postman this morning?'

I'm dumbstruck. I can't believe he's found his way into my other world.

'I'm a hopeless romantic, I just can't help myself. I hope white is your colour. I'm surrendering to you.'

I stand up to establish some semblance of power.

'Look pal, I don't want your flowers and I don't want you following me about.'

He looks genuinely offended.

'I'm not following you, doll. I just popped in to see you.'

'How did you know where I worked? You must have followed me.'

He laughs now, as I erupt internally.

'Are you joking? This is where I first met you, remember? I used to bring in piles of uncorrected proofs when I worked in Thin's.'

'I get a lot of people coming through here. I can't remember.'

'So you took a complete stranger home the other night, you dirty Scottish boy,' he drawls and tries to touch my hand. Pulling away, I fold my arms in front of me defensively.

'Look, please understand. I don't want to get involved with you. My life is complicated enough as it is. No offence mate but please, I'd like you to leave me alone.'

'I'm not averse to affairs. I'm terribly discreet.'

I don't believe this. How can I get it through his thick skull.

'I'm going away. My marriage isn't working out. I'm moving down to London.'

He keeps on.

'A long-distance love affair. I've never been further down than Manchester. Shocking, eh?'

I'm finding it very hard not to lose my cool as I imagine braining the bastard against the counter.

'Will you fucking listen to me? I'm sorry if you think I led you on but Jesus, you pick up a complete stranger in the street and fuck them, what do you expect?'

A blushing schoolboy appears from nowhere and purchases a book on Gallipoli. The creep stands smirking, intensifying the boy's discomfort. What if he tells someone? What if he tells his mother the man in the book shop picks up young guys? The door tings shut again. Creep leans on the counter and in towards me. I back away.

'So when are you leaving then? When can I visit you?'

No more.

'Look, will you fuck off? What do I have to fucking say to you? Get out my fucking face.'

The bastard's lip starts trembling, I don't believe it. A tear runs down his idiot face as he turns and makes for the door, roaring 'cunt' at me as he departs. Never has that word sounded so good.

14

There's no sign of him when I close up at five, so I walk home to reassert my freedom. A couple of times on the way back I imagine I see him in people who look nothing like him. When I turn into Northumberland Street and he's not there, I sense that he could finally have got the message.

As I enter the flat I hear Hope in the living room talking to someone. For a second I imagine the scene in *Fatal Attraction* when gorgeous Michael Douglas comes home and Glenn Close is there pretending she wants to buy the house. Then I hear another female speaking. I pop my head round the door and see Hope sitting with a woman in her thirties and a toddler. The roses are in a vase by the table. Hope gestures to them and smiles.

'Martin dear, this is my niece, Jacqueline, Angus's sister. Get that nice bottle of Chardonnay out the fridge and join us. This is Angus's friend, he's flat-hunting at the moment and being an extremely pleasant house guest in the meantime.'

Telling them I'll be through in a few minutes, I rifle my pockets for my gear as I walk up the hall to my room. I need a joint before I'm subjected to fucking babies.

As it turns out, the child is not too bad. Jacqueline is a crushing bore though. Nobody else wants a drink so I pour myself one and sit in a glorious little stupor, watching the kid doing its kiddish things. It is into everything. Hope seems unconcerned as it staggers around pocketing keys and trying to chew everything in its wake. Is he hyperactive or are they all like this? Jacqueline seems very experienced in the art of sustaining a conversation whilst running about fretting over the wee monster. Jason (and the Argonauts? The Golden Fleece? Surely not Donovan) is playing to an audience and throws a tantrum every time our attention wavers.

After about an hour, and three quarters of a bottle of Chardonnay he starts getting a bit tired and greety. He keeps lolling about the room then crashing into his mother for a cuddle. Hope looks pretty irritated by now. Jacqueline tries to calm him down by shyly singing 'Mockingbird' to him and rocking him gently in her arms. I love croaky, nervous voices like hers, they're so human. 'No sing Mummy, please no sing,' the child pleads. Hope hoots with laughter and the rest of us are soon infected by it. Jason is annoyed that we seem to have got something over on him and starts crying again. Jacqueline notices the renewed look of subdued displeasure on Hope's face and begins getting her things together and squeezing into her coat.

Hope beckons to me as Jacqueline crawls around on the carpet looking for discarded toys. I follow her through to her bedroom. She goes to the other side of the bed, rummages around, puts a bit of wood against the wall and pulls out a wad of notes, counting through them, 20, 40 . . . 180, 190, £200. She slips it in the pocket of her blouse, then tears another twenty off and hands it to me.

'You wouldn't be a dear and pop out and get me a bottle of Ten-Year-Old Macallan's would you? I need to have a word with Jacqueline on her own . . .' she gestures to the money in her pocket, '. . . man trouble,' and winks at me.

She squeezes my hand as she sees me out the flat. Jesus, why was she so obvious about where she keeps money? Is she testing me or something? And £200 to a niece she never sees, just like that. I don't need her money. I don't want it. There's no way I'd steal from her, she's too kind. Stealing is a form of revenge.

As I open the stair door my suppressed trepidation hits me again but the street is still clear. Once I'm sure that nonsense is behind me, I'll be able to put my real feelings for Hope in perspective. It was funny, just the look she gave me tonight when she was telling Jacqueline about me flat-hunting. There are strange erotic sparks between us, I'm sure of it.

When I get back, Jacqueline has gone and Hope is lying back on the settee with *La Traviata* blaring. Her arm rises like a charmed snake and she points at two tumblers on the table. Pulling the Macallan's out the bag, I pour us a couple of measures.

'Straight tonight, madam?'

'Indeed, but twist up one of your little mary-janes as a chaser.'

We lounge back on the settee together, tingle with the whisky and pass the joint to one another as Maria Callas bangs it out. In a matter of days, without trying, our friendship has deepened to such an extent that we feel completely at ease without having to say anything to each other. Nuzzling closer to Hope, she drapes her arm across my shoulders and I snuggle against her upper arm. Her skin smells of talcum and fresh air. The heat where my head touches her arms feels like it's buzzing. I feel utterly replete.

We lie huddled up like this for ages until the CD player clicks and the chorus bursts into '*Dell'invito trescora e' jia' l'ora*', for what must be the second time. Hope clammers up from the settee and switches it off.

Pouring us both another whisky, she gestures to my blow and I obligingly begin rolling another joint.

'Have you ever been to Italy?' I ask as she sits down again.

'La dentro non ci andrei, – pieno di l'Italiani,' she says incomprehensibly in a thick Italian accent. '. . . my husband worked in Rome for a while before I met him but we never made it over together somehow. Maybe he had another wife there.'

The mention of her husband, that tiny part of the vast life she had before I met her, gives me a little twinge of jealousy.

'I'm very backward as far as foreign travel is concerned. Holland once, Greece once, France a few times. I've a couple of pals just outside Paris I see every now and again (eight years ago!). It just seems such a lot of money to spend before you buy your first pint.'

Hope becomes animated.

'Oh I love France – Paris, Fontainebleau, Marseilles . . . Provence used to be lovely too until they BBC'd it and attracted all the riff raff.'

'I'd love to go there with you some time. I could save up.'

Hope waves her hands in front of her like she's doing the Charleston.

'That's a wonderful idea. I'd love a little break. When could you get time off work?'

'I'm owed loads of annual leave but I'm always afraid to take it in case the place goes to pieces without me. Plus, he doesn't pay me when I'm off.'

'Pah, don't worry about money, for God's sake.'

'I'd like to take you, though. If I put a bit away each week we could go there for the next millennium. But you know, I like to pay my own way. I feel bad enough as it is about you not taking anything off me for staying here.'

She dismisses me with a wave of the hand.

'Pay me back a pound a month if it bothers you that much. I'm not going to go hungry without it, put it that way.'

'Oh, but that's terrible.'

She looks at me as if I'm mad.

'What's terrible about it? Is the thought of setting Paris alight with me so awful? Don't be so bloody silly – when could you get time off? In a month? Next week?'

'Whenever, I just need to give a couple of days' notice and my boss can get his wife to watch the place.' I also need time to go through the books with a nit comb.

She bangs her glass against mine.

'Leave it to me. Vive la France.'

We say goodnight at the living room door. Thoughts of a possible free holiday and all the lush times we might have keep me awake for hours. I'm also dying to see Roxanne and Jonathan. We shared a flat for two years when I was studying in London. There's been an open invite since I was last there over eight years ago. Something else always comes up though and work's usually good in the summer as the tourists are such idiots with money.

15

I'm woken up at 2.34 by a right racket out in the street – loud voices, lights flashing through the chinks in the shutters and the roar of machinery. It had better not be those cable TV bastards digging up the road at this time of the morning. I stumble out of bed and over to the window. It's a fucking fire engine, putting out a fire in one of the bins. Such an unbelievable amount of noise for a pissing little fire in a bucket. As I slump back to bed I feel wide awake with anger.

Once I'm back under the duvet, I realise I've left the shutters open but by then I'm getting the fear and don't want to go back over to the window again. Why did a bucket go on fire in a New Town street at half two on a Wednesday morning? It had to be deliberate. Surely that wanker wouldn't pull a stunt like that. The bucket is only about fifteen feet away from the steps up to the flat. He wouldn't, would he? Why am I imagining this? There's been no sign of him since yesterday afternoon. He would have rung the buzzer or been outside when I got home from work. Oh fuck. I bet he's been along at the Phoenix. Fuck fuck fuck. Wild imaginings about the bastard keep me awake for most of the remainder of the night. When the alarm goes off at eight I feel like I've only just shut my eyes.

16

Hope phones me about eleven to say she's booked two open-ended flights to Charles de Gaulle. We can travel any time after tomorrow if there's space on the flights. It's off-peak so we shouldn't have any trouble getting a hotel at the last minute. This time of year it's probably only people over on booze cruises anyway. Hope wants to keep our holiday a secret until we get back in case anyone else tries to get in on the act at the last minute. I can't wait for us to be alone together, to be forced to really get to know one another. If we get on, I am definitely going to go for it.

When I try to phone my boss, I discover he's been in hospital for the past three days – the cancer's gone into his stomach. What'll happen to the shop if he dies? I'd never get another job where I made so much for doing so little. Its almost like this place is part of my identity now. Maybe I should visit him before we go away, see what he's planning to do with it before he pops his clogs. Maybe Hope would buy him out. Mmmh. His daughter, Angela, can't cover for me until next Tuesday though which is a pain in the pisser. Does he have to fucking die when I get the chance of my first holiday in years? I don't tell her where I'm going as I don't want her asking about it when I get back.

I've just put the phone down when it rings again.

'Look Martin, I'm sorry, ok.'

'Who is this?'

'Raymond,' says a hurt-sounding voice.

'Raymond who?'

'The person you told to fuck off yesterday. Have you forgotten me already?'

Oh Jesus, I don't believe it. My hackles are up immediately.

'Look, can I see you? Just once more, please? When are you going away?'

Fuck, how does he know? Then I remember my lie about London.

'Tomorrow, after work, so I really don't have time to meet you.'

'But I need to, sweetheart. You don't understand, I can't see past you . . . I can't think straight.'

Oh, for heaven's sake.

'Look, I'm sorry mate but there's nothing I can do. Give me your address and I'll get in touch when I'm settled.'

'Really? You won't though, will you? I'll never hear from you again. Please Martin, let me see you. I could pop along now. I could help you take your stuff to the station tomorrow . . .'

'No, please, don't come along here. I don't want you in here. Just leave it, for fuck's sake?'

'What time's your train tomorrow? I could meet you at the station. Just five minutes, please?'

It goes on and on like this for about ten minutes. I tell him to fuck off and die and put the phone down on him a couple of times but he just rings back immediately. Why am I tied up in knots by this stupid lie now? Fuck. In desperation, I tell him I'm leaving at six, going from work so I'll be straight on the train. He insists he's going to be there though, no matter what I say he insists and finally hangs up.

Now if I'm not there at six he'll know it was a lie. This

will just go on for fucking ever. I'm actually toying with the idea of saying goodbye, getting on the fucking train for one stop, then coming back again but it seems an absolutely ridiculous thing to have to do for that cunt. If I can just get his focus off Northumberland Street, stop him lurking around so near to Hope. Other than my idea with the train, I can think of no other solution. It is utterly flawed, however, as I'll no doubt bump into the bastard the next day.

Perhaps if I can keep a low profile till we go away next week. Jesus, I can always just take a sickie off work. My attendance record is understandably impeccable and they can't sack me anyway, who would take over? I'm sure Angela would just love to commute from Stirling every day, not. She hates when she has to cover for me. If they have to close the shop and ugly boy goes round there looking for me it'll make my story more convincing.

Spurred on by my own resolve, I phone GNER and book a day return to Berwick on my debit card which I've to pick up at 5.30 tomorrow. I just want this sodding saga cleared up before we go away.

As I close up the shop at five I realise I've forgotten to pilfer anything with all this shit to think about. Hastily scribbling a few books through the ledger that have been on the shelf for months, I take £30 for blow. My booty from yesterday's still in my back pocket and I can go daft for holiday money tomorrow.

Having left the safety of the shop, the unguardedness of the street summons feelings of acute anxiety akin to a massive whitey. Escaping into a taxi, I get the driver to take me to Davie's in Whitson for some gear and to get me out of the stress of the city centre for a while. Fucking £9 as well – I must stop jumping in and out of cabs or else steal my old dear's disabled pass.

Out of politeness I have a couple of joints with Davie, but my nerves are so shot I can only manage a few grunts of conversation. Davie's not much of a talker anyway, it's way too much effort for him. Thank God we have *The Simpsons* on to sustain us. Then I begin getting these involuntary spasms in my left leg and it starts shooting out in front of me. Davie just looks on impassively as if this happens to him all the time. Before long the lack of communication is depressing me so I leave.

As I open the stair door, I see a 21 coming and sprint to the bus stop just in time to save myself from phoning 999 again. As we pull away I see more satellite dishes than I ever have in my life.

Hope is out at a writing workshop when I get back. I'd forgotten all about it but it's convenient. Half-filling two holdalls with books, I stick a few shirts on top, just to give the impression they're full. To avoid having to get them out the house without Hope seeing me in the morning, I put them in the cellar at the bottom of the stair. Although this is probably the stupidest idea I've ever had

I'm trying very hard to get into it, just to see if I can pull it off.

Hope's left me some casserole which looks gorgeous but my hunger is making me nauseous so I place it tactfully in an old bread bag at the bottom of the bin. When was the last time I actually ate anything? I've no idea. I occasionally have a Mars Bar with my coffee at lunchtime but I didn't even manage that this morning. The bottle of Chablis in the fridge, however, is another matter.

It's times like this I really miss having a telly. Without such a distraction I'm soon worrying about everything again and my proposed plan of action seems sillier, the more I think about it.

When Hope comes in at midnight, I'm sitting dozing on the settee, exhausted by my procrastination earlier. Leaning over me, she kisses my forehead. The smell of whisky on her breath explains her wide-awake radiance.

'The tutor didn't turn up so we all went to a pub, I'm quite pissed. A real man's bar, it was . . . I liked it. Real people can be frightfully entertaining sometimes. They just come out with it, don't they?'

Feelings of animosity towards whoever she's been out with start bouncing around inside my head. Why didn't she phone to say where she was? I'd have phoned her and invited her to join me. Stop it, stop it. Why am I getting like this. I've not even shagged her yet?

'I'm on annual leave from tomorrow night,' I lie, whitely.

Hope claps her hands together.

'That's wonderful.' She looks at her watch, 'Oh, I suppose it's too late to phone the airport now, isn't it?'

And whose fault is that?

'There's a couple of things I have to do before we go anyway. How about Saturday, if there's flights available?'

'Fine by me. I'll call a couple of hotels I know in the morning. Super. Anyway, you're not going to believe some of the things I overheard in that pub . . .'

I've no desire to hear about her new pals. Her enthusiasm for them is stressing me out. I stroke my temples melodramatically.

'Sorry, Hope, I've had this migraine coming on for the last half hour. I'm going to have to lie down. Tell me tomorrow, eh?'

She pretends to look hurt. God, I hate the mind fucks you give yourself when you're emotionally involved with someone.

'Poor dear. There's some out-of-date DF118s in the bathroom cabinet if they'd help.'

DF118s! I don't really have a migraine but I help myself to six, swallow two and put the rest in a little inkwell in my room. It feels wonderful to be in bed. If I could just stay here for a few months. That's what I'll do on Friday, keep a low profile. Will she book single rooms or a double I wonder? She didn't even ask me. If I just think of it all as an adventure. It is an adventure. The thing at the station tomorrow is part of it. It's sort of exciting, I suppose. The DFs start to take hold really quickly. I'm having really disgusting fantasies about Hope by the time I fall asleep.

17

In the morning, she's not up (no doubt hungover) by the time I go to work. I leave a note on the telephone table saying, 'back late' – deliberately unspecific to get her back for not calling last night. Only taking enough money with me for a taxi, I count through the rest – £440. That's not forgetting the two grand in my Savings Account. 'This is going to be some fucking holiday' I think as I stuff the wad in a sock.

Having retrieved my holdalls from the cellar, I struggle out with them, feeling stupider by the second. As I turn into the positively mountainous Dublin Street, my arms are aching from the ridiculously heavy bags. Taxis are whizzing by on Queen Street but I have to scale the worst of it before I finally manage to stop one.

Work is a nightmare, as I have to square the place up, make the accounts looks semi-respectable, run through loads of fucking figures to make sure I've covered myself on everything. Every time the door goes I feel like Anne Frank. There's loads of students in during the morning, giggling, talking very loud and constantly asking for things, making me work my arse off for piddling little £1.50 paperbacks.

By mid-afternoon I've not managed to make a penny

for myself. A guy comes in with a carrier bag full of photography books – Ansen Adams, Weegee, Cartier-Bresson, but I can't find a fucking pencil anywhere. He lends me his pen and I know I'm going to have to make at least £100 or nothing at all on the deal. Utterly offended by my initial offer of a tenner, he says something like £90. Although the books are worth five times that, this could be my only chance of the day. It takes me about twenty minutes to haggle him down to £25. I respect him for holding out so long but business is business. I'm wasted in this job, I should be on Wall Street.

Any empathy I had with the guy disappears when I notice he's put the figure in the book himself, when he was signing it. Fuck, there's barely room for a '1' in there and I was counting on a '2'. I'll need to watch him if he comes in again. He's probably worked in a bookshop and knows the form. It's nearly half three by the time he leaves and I still have to do something with all the books I've been buying and not bothering to display for the past few months. I'm sweating like a bastard by the time I close up at five, a mere hundred pounds richer.

The stupid bloody bags mean I have to get yet another taxi to the station. It'll be worth it though, if it gets that bastard off my back, at least until he's calmed down about the whole thing. It should flatter me that someone's so into me, but I'm from Edinburgh, you know, I hate people invading my space.

There's a long queue at the booking office. I should have told the bastard to stand in the queue for me while he was waiting, although he doesn't seem to be here yet, anyway. That's fine though, the less time I have to spend with him the better.

I'm in a queue for ten minutes before I realise there's a separate desk for previously paid-for tickets. They serve me immediately as apparently no-one else has the savvy to pay in advance.

Leaving the booking hall, I walk down to the platform, but still can't see him. In WH Smith's, I thumb the glossies for ten minutes, then for extra authenticity, buy a copy of *Time Out.* Still no sign. It's now 5.45. Walking round to the Rendezvous Point, I scan the crowd and sit down. The smell from the bin next to me turns my stomach. I walk back over to the platform. The tannoy announces that the train is arriving. Lots of people waiting, but not him.

At 5.52 I walk back over to the shop, then have another quick look in the booking hall. Jesus, I don't believe this, I'm going to fucking Berwick for his benefit and he's not even here. What will I do? I've wasted £15 on a fucking ticket. This isn't on.

5.58 and people are getting on the train, doors are being slammed, the engine is starting to roar. Will I just go home? Stand in that fucking queue again to get a refund on my ticket? What if he's watching me? That's it, he's fucking watching to see if I go or not.

The guard asks me if I'm getting on. I stand like a bewildered prick for a few seconds, then he asks me again. Utterly humiliated, I jump on. The door is slammed behind me and the fucking train is off before I even have time to think about it.

Clambering up to the smoking carriage in complete shock, I drop into a seat and light up a Silk Cut. As Edinburgh slowly disappears, I still can't quite believe what I'm doing. The whole journey down I'm raging at myself for doing something so fucking idiotic. It's an hour's wait at Berwick to get the train back, and once I'm on it I crash out, sick of thinking.

It's only thanks to some noisy squaddies getting on at Waverley that my evening doesn't end in Aberdeen. Then I'm hawking those bloody bags back down the bloody platform again, thinking that if I see him now I'll fucking kill myself. I try phoning the flat but there's no answer.

It's nine o'clock by the time I get my third taxi of the day. I must learn to drive, I hate having to rely on these fuckers. As I get dropped off I'm relieved to see that the lights are all off in the flat, so I can get the bags in again undetected.

My note to Hope has gone from the telephone table, but there's an envelope with my name on it – just 'Martin'. It's definitely not Hope's flamboyant script, in fact I know exactly who it's from the second I see it. He must have put it through the fucking door. Please make Hope have been out when he turned up. There's no note to say where she is and it makes me feel stupid for bothering to tell her I'd be late. Taking the envelope through to my room I need a joint before I can face it.

There's a flimsy bit of lined paper, torn out of a notebook, inside, folded once. All that is written on it is 'vous l'avez voulu'. What the fuck does that mean? Why didn't I nick a French phrasebook from work for next week? Has he found out about Paris? How long has it been lying there? Maybe he couldn't make it to the station. Why would he bring it here though, if he thought I'd be gone? Please don't let Hope have met him. I don't want to have to explain him to her.

Looking out onto the empty street as I finish the joint, it begins to really irritate me that Hope hasn't left me a note. Maybe she phoned while I was out. Going into the hall, I do a 1471 but it's the fucking pay phone I called from at the station.

Thinking she might have left a note in the living room, I open the door. A black shape lunges at me from nowhere. The shock knocks me over. The next thing I'm aware of is something licking my face. It's his dog. It's his fucking dog. He's fucking in here.

Thrusting myself into the room, I expect him to be sitting there with a fucking smug look on his face but it's empty. There are cushions all over the floor and it smells of piss. My whole body begins trembling, like I'm going to have a fit, as I stagger up and check the kitchen, then the bathroom.

They are both in Hope's bed. As I walk round taking it all in, it seems strangely normal. Hope's skin is yellow and plastic-looking, her throat discoloured by what looks like a string of lovebites. They are the same colour as the inordinately large tongue which lollops at the side of her mouth. Her eyes are open and pleading with me to do something. I close them.

Raymond is lying sideways over her. His skin is much darker than hers but yellow still seeps through. A huge, wet, purple carnation blossoms out on the blue sheet beneath his hand. The dog jumps up on the bed and tries to lick the death from his face. It is like something out of a Japanese horror film. I think about the air tickets on the mantelpiece and the money under the floor. I think about calling Shirley, or dialling 999. Then I think about me being just another cunt getting carted into a prison van on the Scottish news. Nah, I don't think so.

The Happening

I WAKE WITH the cold, tight-headed, empty sense of an impending family day. Annual leave is precious and it galls me to waste any of it with cousins' brats, my foul auntie and my mother's inevitable tears after a few glasses of Asti Spumante.

There's an unpleasant and unfamiliar odour in the bed beside me. Rolling onto my back, I feel too warm. The side of my thigh suddenly touches flesh, the slight contact eliciting a grunt from someone at my side. Gently retrieving my leg, I lie rigid, trying to recall something, anything. It's not until I hear the burr of light snoring that I can bear to look. Extremely hazy recollections of the latter part of the office party make this almost unbearable.

Who the hell is that? There's a teenage boy in my bed. A smelly angel with a dirty face. I haven't been in bed with a teenage boy since the neighbour's son used to babysit when I was nine. What the fuck is going on? Afraid to move or breathe, I wonder if this is what being scared stiff feels like. It's not just the fact that my bedmate could be anyone – a sleepy burglar, a sensitive rapist – it's trying to remember what happened and none of it explaining this.

There was the thing at work. God knows how much wine I had with lunch before moving onto serious G&Ts. Socialising with colleagues always puts me terribly on edge. Outwith our work roles it's as if we're complete strangers. Did I ask Bob about promotion? Oh Jesus. I've just had this vision of Marion, Bob and I in the Bistro. How did we get there? Didn't Bob buy champagne and keep trying to snog me? I definitely remember cold, wet lips bearing down. Beyond that there's just this bad, scary feeling.

Quietly extricating myself from the bed I stare at the boy. Is he naked? Not really wanting to know I nonetheless lift the duvet a little and stare underneath. He is naked – slim, pale, beautiful, dirty and naked. He'll think I'm a pervert if he suddenly wakes up, but despite this, I can't seem to stop looking. Have I already had him?

Reluctantly curtailing my voyeurism, I trace a path of clothes to the living room. My bra and screwed-up dress entwined, muddy Dr Martens, Superman tights (sunny-side up), dirty Levi's encasing suspect yellow-stained white Y-fronts. Checking he's still asleep I rifle the pockets of his inordinately heavy jeans for some clue to his identity. A mobile number scribbled on a betting slip looks vaguely familiar. Whose number starts 0774? Evelyn's? The front pockets are so crammed with coins they can't even muster a rattle as I search. I find a packet of Rizlas and a lump of hash wrapped in a rag of tinfoil in the little pocket at the front. Then I think I hear a noise from the bedroom and haphazardly stuff everything back.

'Hello,' I endeavour, shakily. No response. When I go through to the bedroom he's still snoring. Closing the door quietly behind me I accost the phone. It's no good, I'll have to pick Marion's brains. I'll be cagey, though, as I hate confessing to blackouts. People fill your memory gaps with things they can use against you. Never get drunk with work-mates. I'm always telling myself that. I dial the number.

It's worse than I thought. Marion tries to say I dragged Bob, my boss, shy-Helen-the-Finance-Officer and her to the Bistro. They supposedly had other things arranged but I became persuasively aggressive. I knew she'd make up bull-shit like that. Bob and I were allegedly all over each other. Helen left because he tried to neck her on the way back from the Ladies.

'He actually offered us a lift. After what, about a litre of Grouse and that bloody champagne. Unbelievable. And remember him grabbing that girl's breast at the bar? Why didn't they chuck us out?'

'Pretty excruciating,' I agree, clueless.

'Sorry Cath. You know I was going to come for the meal but after all his shite with the waitress, God, why do people like that drink?'

'The three of us went to a restaurant?'

'You what?'

'I mean just you, me and Bob?'

'Don't you remember? I left before we got a table. Did you stay for the meal? God Cath, how could you? Did he keep trying it on?'

Jesus, this isn't making any sense. Mystery boy will wake up at this rate.

'No Marion, see, it's just like . . . well . . . I met someone. Was anyone else with us when you left?'

She laughs. 'What, a man?'

'Yes.'

'Is he there now? Sure it's not Bob? I thought I was going to have to throw a bucket of water over the pair of you.'

'Oh please, I feel sick enough as it is.'

'So what happened? Did you shag this bloke?'

This is hopeless.

'Look Cath, I better go, I have to get into mother-mode. Merry bloody Christmas.'

'Not as merry as yours by the sounds of it.'

Putting the phone down, I go back through to the bedroom. Rummaging in the bedside table for my Prozac, I'm aware of the duvet at my side, moving.

'Morning, gorgeous!'

Grabbing my wrist, he pulls me gently towards him and gives me a grubby kiss. I recoil at the smell of me on his breath. He flutters his long eyelashes, sleepily.

'Thanks for letting me stay.'

I'm aghast. A man is actually thanking me for sleeping with him and I've no idea who he is.

Ruffling his spiky hair he asks if he can have a wash. His request makes him blush. Pointing out the shower, I get a couple of bath towels from the airing cupboard. Once I hear the water going on I start picking up his things, folding clothes over the arm of the settee, then moving them to the upright chair when I realise how filthy they are. I take the cannabis out of his pocket again. By now the tinfoil has effectively disintegrated. I loved getting stoned when I was younger, but all my friends are straight these days, sobered up by childbirth. Impulsively I bite a bit off, smoothing the teeth-marks with my finger and hide it amidst the Christmas cards.

Anticipating a silence when he gets out, I switch on the television – cartoons, a sickly American children's film, a throng of singing Christians, or the fuzz of Channel 5. Switching it off, I go to make some coffee.

Did we meet him in the restaurant? Surely they wouldn't let someone that dirty into a place where people eat? I remember Bob standing with his raincoat on. Did he leave when the urchin appeared? Where the fuck did he come from?

A vision in steam, naked to the waist comes out of the bathroom. Beneath the grime he is even more beautiful. I invite him through to the kitchen for coffee. He has a lovely smile.

Sitting opposite each other, I watch him spoon four sugars into his mug. Taking a cigarette from a packet on the table, he offers me one. Where did they come from? Were we through here last night? Why can't I remember?

'Or do you fancy a Christmas spliff?'

Oh no, the blow.

'I don't mind.'

Retrieving his jeans, he comes back, fumbling through them. What if he notices they've been interfered with? He'll see teeth-marks on his dope, I know he will.

'I should have a wee bit left,' he says, taking it from his pocket. Oh God, he's noticed. 'Aye fine, plenty,' he reassures, proceeding to roll a joint.

Let him do the talking. He has an unfair advantage – he knows what happened and I don't. He looks up as he crumbles hash.

'Have you recovered then?'

'From what?' I ask tentatively. He raises his eyebrows and grins.

'Last night.'

'I was pretty drunk,' I explain, but it is really a question.

'I think we all were.'

'All?'

He shuts his eyes and looks like he's imagining something extremely amusing then hands me the joint. Lighting up, I inhale deeply. Maybe this'll help me work up the nerve to ask him. Oh, but I can't admit not remembering whether we had sex. I'd be devastated if someone said that to me.

'No offence or anything, but I didn't think much of your mate.'

'What mate?' Was Marion lying to me. Was she here?

'Bob, wasn't it?'

'Bob, my boss?'

'Boss?' he chuckles in seeming disbelief.

'What about him? What was wrong with him?'

He looks at me as if I'm mad.

'Strangely enough, the recovery position for someone having an epileptic fit isn't throwing them out in the snow. Thanks for letting me back in, I felt terrible. Someone stole my medication when I was sleeping.'

I return the joint to him, even more confused now.

'Where? Here? Someone pinched your medicine when you were here?'

'No, outside the shop, where you met me.'

'What do you mean?'

'Argos, my room-with-a-view, you know? Phenobarbitones too. They'll end up having a fit themselves. Divine retribution, I suppose.'

'Sorry, I still don't understand.'

'That's where I sleep. It's compact but it's home, you know.'

My jaw does a Gordon Brown. There's a homeless person sitting opposite me, a fucking down-and-out, drinking my

Gold Blend. I picked up a dosser outside Argos in front of my fucking boss? This is ludicrous. 'When did Bob leave?'

He's obviously amused that I can't remember.

'You threw him out after he tried to throw me out. You were great, my hero.' He crosses his heart with his hands.

That's maybe not so bad. Bob was so pissed he was probably completely obnoxious. How could I forget someone having an epileptic fit on my carpet, though? Please make Bob have left before anything happened between me and the Artful Dodger. I don't even know his name and can't conceivably ask now. Downing my coffee I take the mug over to the sink, lightheaded from the drugs. He offers me another puff and I decline.

'No, no thanks. I'm going to have to get my act together. I'm going to my mother's. How about yourself?'

He shrugs, finishes his coffee and goes to get dressed. When he returns, I can't stand it any more, I have to know.

'So where did we meet you? I don't mean to be rude but my memory's gone.'

Blushing again, he pulls on his filthy combat jacket.

'I asked you for money. Your pal invited me for a meal with the pair of you. He said if he gave me money I'd spend it on drugs. I've not had a proper meal in weeks, so thanks. It was my Christmas dinner, I suppose.'

What a patronising bastard Bob is. What must they have thought in the restaurant? Two extremely drunk businesspeople and a tramp. To my relief he walks towards the door.

I'd feel such a heel having to ask him to leave if he's just going to be sitting in a shop doorway for the day. God, I've shagged a homeless person.

He kisses me as I unlock the door. Soap disguises the sex smell from earlier.

'Thanks for everything, pet. I don't suppose you'll want to see me again, but I want you to know, you're a really kind person.'

Could it be that innocent? Have I actually done something extremely charitable? Bought a homeless man a meal, saved him from having a fit in the snow, let him stay at my house on Christmas Eve and given him what was probably his first fuck in years.

'I'll know where to find you if I do,' I say, making a mental note never to walk up the North Bridge after dark again. As I wish him Merry Christmas and begin closing the door, he suddenly looks extremely perplexed. Don't let him ask if he can stay, please.

'One thing. I have to say it. I'm sorry.'

Dread renders me incapable of responding.

'It's just . . . I would have preferred if it had just been you and me, you know, not the three of us. I only joined in because you asked me to. I don't usually go with guys. You won't think any less of me, will you?'

Castle Terrace Car Park

KEN. PERFECT NAME for the bastard. If he wasn't English, he'd say it all the time – ken this, ken that, ken what you mean. Always something to fucking say. Always some meaningless fact or opinion to share. But he's my boss, so every two months we have to go through this round-for-dinner crap. I don't know why we bother. I haven't had so much as a sniff at promotion for nearly five years. Ken. Love him. Love to boot him to oblivion. God knows what Barbara sees in him. He's got a face like an aborted pig's foetus.

He's on his second plate of Karen's homemade moussaka. The first helpings were Desperate Dan-sized but the rotund one obviously doesn't get fed properly at home, so is making the most of it. From what I hear, Barbara doesn't take any of her wifely obligations too seriously. Who can blame her? Living with that human wheelie bin.

'Uh, Karen, this is really delicious. I don't normally eat

aubergines but these are just perfect. What's the herb, that really nice flavour?'

Karen rewards his culinary compliment by topping up his glass. He puts his hand over it as it nears the brim and she pours some red wine on it. Stupid prick.

'Oh, sorry,' she wipes it with a napkin, giggling like a teenager. 'It's rosemary. That's the only seasoning in it. No garlic or anything.'

Of course it's fucking rosemary. Everyone knows that rosemary is the major ingredient in moussaka. Why are they having this non-conversation? Jesus, must he eat with his mouth full? I feel like I can see every calorie making its journey to join his already prodigious blubber.

The wine-spilling incident has Barbara giggling away as well now. It's like a bloody chimp's tea party. I quite fancied Barbara as well, but I hate seeing people laughing about nothing. They're like lemmings. And now Ken's started as well. That's it. It's like that old Smash commercial from the seventies. For Mash get Smashed. I hate that he's in some way got both the bitches laughing. I feel like sticking my fork in his eye.

Once Ken's finished his second, mammoth helping, Karen clears the plates away and the room descends into a silence, punctuated only by him still fannying on about how wonderful the meal was. We agree to have a break before pudding. It probably breaks Ken's heart, but he's already proved himself to be a supreme greedy cunt, so he goes with the status quo. We go through to the living room, so we can open up the patio door for Barbara to have a cigarette. I suggest putting on some music, so I have something decent to listen to. Ken's on his feet and over at the CD player.

'I'll pick something, d'you mind? Or any requests?'

That he drops dead. Fuck, I hate having my choice of music undermined. He knows how sensitive I am about it. I spend more than £50 a week in Fopp. I read *Select*, *NME*, *Mojo*, *Q*. I download music endlessly off the net. I pride myself on keeping my finger on the musical pulse. All for that fat twat to barge in and put on, fucking hell, this pure pish 60s compilation I only parted with £1.99 for in the post office because it had Peter Sarstedt's 'Where Do you Go to my Lovely' on it, and that jumps. Christ. Bastard. A few thousand quid's worth of up-to-the-minute compact discs and I'm going to be branded a fucking Gerry and the Pacemakers fan. How much do I hate this cunt?

It's not even the original recordings. It's one of these Now We Are Sixty efforts where the artistes that haven't, in the intervening years, either died of Parkinsons or alcoholism get invited in to re-record their hits in an unrecognisable fashion for the price of a packet of incontinence pads. Fucking hell. Gerry Marsden. 'I Like It'.

Ken and Karen take an armchair each. I bring a dining-room chair through and sit behind them, so I can see Barbara. There's a breeze and she keeps having to push her hair out of her eyes. She's got these intense fucking eyes.

She sucks on her cigarette, in a dream. I glance at her, trying to work out if I can see a panty line or not, wonder who goes on top with her and fat boy and think about her putting these full, pink lips round my big pink one. She's fucking hot. I decide at that moment that I'm going to fuck her. That will be my next project. My last one was Karen's sister. Frigid bitch that she was, I shouldn't have wasted my fucking time.

In conjunction with me silently pledging to fuck his wife, Ken croons, badly, the intro to Billy J Kramer's 'Bad To Me'.

'If you ever leave me,
I'll be sad and blue,
don't you ever leave me,
I'm so in love with you,' he warbles, eyebrows raised hopefully at Barbara. She nods her head, obviously embarrassed. Twat.

With Barbara completely uninterested, Ken goes back to talking to Karen, about some fucking company he's bought shares in that's doing well. Never thought to let me in on who they were, when it was only 28p a share. He's made about twenty grand in the last month. Won't shut up about it. I hope the stock market crashes.

Barbara stubs her fag under the toe of her black, leather boot, then comes back in and locks the patio doors. I'd complain to anyone else for making the place look like a Wester Hailes bus stop, but like the idea of having her lipstick on a fag butt in my garden. I stand up to go over and sit on the settee beside her, but she hunches down in front of Ken and sits between his legs. It's repugnant. What's she fucking playing at? She's not been giving him the goods for months. He told me himself. I hate couples that put on some lovey-fucking-dovey act in public but in private wank themselves raw and don't speak to each other for weeks on end. I feel quietly gutted. Still, her undignified position on the floor forces the slit in her skirt open, so I just sit in silence and imagine sliding my head between her beefy thighs, as Ken waffles on.

The only person who actually seems to be listening to him is Karen. Karen, for some unfathomable reason, appears to like the guy. She laughs at the feeblest so-called funny anecdotes and observations, always finds some alternative thread to pull out of all his conversations and they seem to have a lot of wee in-jokes together. I work with the guy, but she seems closer to him, more intimate.

Karen's like that, though. She lets very few people into her world, but when she does, she quickly creates an individual little cosmos with that person. Like a magnet that only has the power to attract one thing at a time. Subsequently, Barbara's a bit left out and has a wonderful, off-fucking-someone-else-in-my-head look about her. It makes me feel better about her sitting between Ken's flabby thighs. Well, not exactly better. Just less bad. I catch her eye a few times and she gives me a noncommittal smile. She wants me. It's not like she's fucking Ken. Hot woman like that must be getting it somewhere, you know. She must be fair game. The split skirt says it all.

She must be a handful in one way or another. Why else would Ken tell me, and anyone else at work that would listen, that she wouldn't let him touch her? His gonads are obviously so full it's affecting his sense of decorum and common decency. Jesus, if I was married to a sexy whore like that, and she wasn't giving me the goods, d'you think I'd be admitting it to people? She'd be getting it up the arse on a daily basis as far as anyone else I knew was concerned. Imagine admitting that your wife doesn't even fancy you. How can you respect someone like that?

Barbara gets up to go to the toilet. Her skirt opens wide so I can see right up to the top of her leg. She's not wearing stockings or anything, but it still gives me a semi. In a split second, I imagine that big fucking arse of hers squashed on every part of my body. Jesus. She's so hot I feel like just fucking grabbing her in front of them and giving her one. Don't even give anyone time to protest. Just for a moment, I want her so much, I'd risk my job, marriage, home, getting charged with rape, to just fuck her over the Omni Pine coffee table. Karen and Ken watching would just make it better. That's the ironic thing. How does life have to be full of such boring rules and conventions? How fantastic would it be if I could just fuck any woman, whenever and wherever I felt like it?

Ken's leaning over her now, arms round her from behind, kissing her hair.

'It's our seventh anniversary tomorrow, isn't it love?'

Barbara wriggles forward for some space. Pulls a face that implies tolerance, but I read loathing.

'So that's what that itch is,' she sneers, then spoils it all by turning round and kissing the bastard. It makes me feel like I've stubbed my toe; my little toe. The same rush of rage you get. I look at Karen to ground myself. She looks as pissed off as me. What for, I'm not too fucking sure. Nah, she'd never fancy him. What am I thinking? Fucking gut-bucket like that. It's just her weird fucking way. Why I can still be bothered with her after all these years, I suppose. It's never boring cos she's so fucking weird. Plus, she just hates that fucking couple shite as well. It's always just a cover for profound antagonism.

I need to break my sense of them being the focus of the whole room. The only track I like on the CD, the Peter Sarstedt one, is on and I don't want my liking of it violated by an image of whale-boy fondling my next fuck. I fill up my glass, no-one else's, take it over to the CD rack with me, and pull out some Beethoven sonatas CD I've not played in years. Make Billy-fucking-Fury feel a bit inadequate. Though Karen's started flirting with him again, while she thinks my back's turned, so I'm not so sure.

The settee's empty, but I go back over and sit on the dining chair, so I can keep my delightful vigil on Barbara's split.

'*The Pathetique*, isn't it?' says Ken suddenly, like a spider running across my face and waking me up.

I know it is, or probably is, because there's only three sonatas on that CD and that's probably one of them, but the fact that Ken knows this scunners me. I probably pull the sort of face you would when you're told after thirty-seven years that your father was really Hughie Green. How does that do-wah-diddy-diddy cunt know that anyway? He's fucking pathetique. Christ, I almost said it out loud there. How much wine have I had. Three quarters of a bottle. Nah, I'm fine.

I refill my own glass, then go through to the kitchen for another bottle. I just need away from that prick for a minute or two. God, what's wrong with me tonight? He doesn't usually wind me up this much. We spend all day at work together, and in that environment he's all right. I actually do quite like him, within reason. It's just when he's on my own territory he automatically puts my back up. My stomach's starting to churn now. Better take some Pepto-Bismol.

I've just taken a swig, and let out a belch, when Barbara comes into the kitchen, wanting painkillers. Well, supposedly wanting painkillers, but she's giving me that direct stare of hers and her hands are on the back of her hips. I start rummaging through cupboards, knowing full well that the Nurofen are in the kitchen drawer.

'It's him gives me the headaches. Not the booze. See

when he gets going on a subject, he just seems to lose all sense of how boring he can be,' she whispers, smiling at our little secret.

I stop hunting pills and lean against the sink beside her. She looks slightly surprised at my suddenly standing so close to her but doesn't move away, just keeps flashing that come-on of a smile of hers. I reason quickly in my head. I only see her when Karen and I have dinner with the pair of them, she's offering me it on a plate here, and I want to get my own back on her old man, anyway. Plus wine always helps.

'Well, if it ever gets too boring and you want someone to talk to . . .'

'How d'you mean?'

Bitch, she's going to make me work for it.

'You know. Just to chat, or more, or whatever. I only ever get the chance to see you on nights like this. I'd like to see you on your own, sometime.'

She looks bemused, but her defences are down. She's leaning against the bunker now, nipples out and pointing at me. The only part of her showing the slightest resistance is her gob.

'Chat, or more? What do you mean exactly?'

'Whatever you want it to mean. No pressure or anything. Just, I think there's something going on between us, and we should maybe meet up and talk about it.'

I take a slug of my wine, buoyed by my nerve in just coming out with it. Women love that. They hate when a man beats about the bush and expects them to do all the running.

'Between us? You mean you and me?'

'C'mon Barbara, tell me it's my imagination we've been eyeing each other up through there for the past three hours.'

Her smile warms again and I know I've hit a raw nerve.

'I thought I had something on my chin,' she giggles, boring into me with these incredible bloody blue eyes of hers. Someone's going to come through in a minute if I don't do something quick. I grab her hand and pull her towards me, aiming my lips at hers. Next thing I'm aware of is a pain in my cheekbone, a mug clattering on the floor and her vanished back through. Fuck. She fucking hit me. I can't believe it. I'm reeling, not so much from being hit, but by the shock of her response. My cock's straining in my pants. Now I really want to fuck her.

But I need to get myself together. What if she's through there at this moment, telling them all I just made a grab at her. I put my hand up to my face, to check for blood but it seems ok. It was just a dunt. If she'd meant it, I'd be out cold.

I'm just about to go back through and face the music, when Karen comes barging in with a look that requires an explanation from me.

'What are you doing through here? Don't leave me with Ken, eh? He's your boss. How come I always end up with him bending my ear?'

Phew.

'You seem to like it. I can't get a word in edgeways once you pair start your mutual appreciation society crap.'

'Oh, come off it, eh. I'm just being polite. Someone around here has to. We're just trying to keep the conversation going because you're not making any bloody effort. And stop snapping at the poor guy, for God's sake.'

I drain my glass, and pour another. 'Yeah, Karen, sure. Just doing your good hostess bit. Of course. How didn't I realise? How could I think you were just slobbering over each other?'

Karen grabs the bottle off me and pours herself another. 'Oh yeah, Brian. Spot on. I've just been sitting thinking about sucking on his big dick all night. Yeah. Obesity in a man really makes me moist. Get a fucking life, eh?' and she storms back through.

Getting a couple of Nurofen from the kitchen drawer, I follow her. Ken is still talking, oblivious. Barbara is sitting behind him in the dining-room chair I was sitting in earlier. Her legs are out again. Is it a peace offering, or is she just offering me a piece? Karen's hunched up on the settee in a grand huff. I just want to go to bed and have a wank, but instead I take the armchair and go into a dream as one of Ken's soliloquies drones on in the background. Karen says very little and leaves the few brief awkward silences there are for me to fill in. Barbara just looks pissed off, but she never usually says much anyway. You must just get past it after a while, living with that non-stop gobshite. She doesn't smile again for the rest of the evening, though. She doesn't look as attractive when she's not smiling. She just looks like a sour-faced, craggy dyke like the rest of them. I can't stand moody bitches like that. Maybe I got off lightly. I shouldn't imagine she'll tell him about our fracas in the kitchen, but even if she did, the bastard's so soft, he'll probably think she was just over-reacting.

We all suffer about another two hours of it, then Ken says they better go, work in the morning and all that shit. It's only 10.30 but I suppose something that big needs a lot of rest. We see them off at the door. Barbara looks fucking radiant in the fresh, night air, it must be said. I think about fucking her over the bonnet of my car in Castle Terrace car park, then say goodnight and close the door.

Karen gives me the silent treatment as we clean up. The dishes just go in the microwave, to hide them. I blitz the living room with a bin bag then put it outside for the morning. When I go back in, Karen's sitting on the settee, with her head back and a large gin and tonic in her hand.

'Jesus, can that man talk. I don't know how Barbara can put up with him. Is he like that all the time? At work and that?'

I get myself a bottle of Beck's and sit on the settee beside her with my legs over hers.

'I think it's just the captive audience sets him off.'

She looks at me daggers.

'Hey, don't start that again. Bloody cheek you've got, honestly, Brian. Leave me to entertain your bloody boss, then accuse me of coming on to him because I bothered to try and engage him in conversation.'

I stroke her hair, 'I know. I know. I'm just winding you up. Thanks for that. It's more than that torn-faced bitch, Barbara, did. She barely fucking spoke all night. Is she catatonic or something?'

Karen sips her drink.

'I quite like her. I like her take on things.'

'But you hardly spoke to her all night. Nah, Karen. She's a prize bitch. Best avoided.'

She shrugs, finishes her drink and goes through to the bedroom. I generally spend a wee while on the chatrooms to unwind before bed, but I'm still quite horny from Ms Ice Queen going sadistic on me. I already have my fantasy worked out. I've been honing it to perfection for the last two hours, for fuck's sake.

I clean my teeth, then strip in the bathroom and go through to join Karen. She's lying on her stomach. The light's already off. I enter the duvet from the bottom, crawling underneath until I'm hunched round her back.

'Fuck!'

'What?'

'I forgot to give them the bloody rhubarb confit.'

Whilst it's not the most alluring pre-love talk I've ever heard, I bite at her shoulders a bit, then push in and start to fuck her regardless. As usual, she's soon on her knees and pushing back to meet me. I can hear her slurping as I slide in and out. I'm back in Castle Terrace car park. Barbara's just getting out of her car, and I grab her from behind. She struggles in my grasp and elbows me in the eye, but it just gives me a rush of adrenaline and extra strength to push her, face down, over the car bonnet, pull her knickers to the side and ram it up her arse. I have to put my hand over her mouth to stifle her screams. She bites at my fingers as her sphincter tugs at my cock. I pull them away, push them up her blouse and squeeze her nipples until she screams, then pull out and shoot my load up the back of her raincoat.

I fall off Karen onto my back, come still oozing from me. She finishes off, then calls me a bastard. A minute later she's snoring. Selfish bitches. The lot of them.

Reanimation

THE OTHER DAY I killed a wasp. Chloe threw a hideous tantrum as it had been trying to speak to her and the room was suddenly quiet. She stormed to her room and refused to get out from under the duvet 'til the following evening. Her mother used to do the same thing, even before the illness. Sometimes I pretend that she is still just in the other room.

Yesterday morning, when I took up Chloe's breakfast, she shoved something under the bed in a fluster.

'I'm tidying my room,' she insisted, her eyes guilty and everywhere. I put the glass of milk and peanut butter sandwich on the floor by the door and tried to approach her. She flew at me, trying to push me out the room.

'Please daddy, go away. I'll tell you when it's ready.'

As she punched at my arms and stomach, I wanted to cry. Not just because the strength of her rebuke shocked me, but because she has a secret. Already, at only six years old, there are things she doesn't want her daddy to know.

I barked at the photo of Tricia on the dresser in our room. I sat on our bed – sulky, angry and numb – hating her and everything. I pretended to respect her decision not to go for the second course of chemo, but it just seems like the ultimate selfishness now, as if she didn't really give a damn about either of us. Then I hated myself even more for thinking that because I know it's so utterly untrue.

After a while, I sensed Chloe watching me from the doorway. I looked up from my hunched position on the bed. Her eyes were burning into me, telling me to take a look at myself; telling me I was no sort of support in the state I was in. Then she walked in and gave me a hug and asked if she could watch her *Shrek* video.

'Tell you what, Chlo – you go downstairs and get the biscuit tin and the video on, and we'll sit and watch it together, ok? How about that?'

'Oh-kay' she sing-songed wearily, like she'd be doing me a huge favour.

I followed her out the room and watched her walking backwards down the stairs.

'Stop that, Chloe. You'll hurt yourself.'

Another piercing glower, a humph and she turned away from me and tore down the stairs, screaming.

Waiting 'til I heard the television going on, I sneaked into her room and knelt beside the bed, grasping underneath for the source of her secrecy. Months of unhoovered carpet fluff and skin flakes reared up in front of me, prickling the inside of my nostrils as I pulled out trainers, dolls, comics and discarded presents we'd bought her.

'Daddy, *Shrek's* starting,' she yelled up the stairs.

'Just pause it. I'll be down in a second, sweetheart,' I snuffled, accidentally breathing in a cloud of floating dust. Despite my sneezing fit, I kept fumbling about blindly under the bed, until Tricia's old vanity case was on the carpet beside me. Tricia always kept it at the side of the dressing table in our room. I hadn't noticed it was gone.

Feeling foolish I started to chuck all the debris back under the bed. All young girls like to experiment with their mum's make-up. Better Chloe get use out of it than it lie unnoticed in our room like some cosmetic catacomb. Nostalgically, I clipped open the fastener and opened it up. My shriek had Chloe straight back up the stairs, hitting me again as she tried to pull the ghastly, makeshift graveyard away from me.

'That's mine! Gimme it Daddy, it's mine,' she wailed as I blocked her with my back, fingering through the case in horror. A bird, rotten with maggots; numerous blue bottles and wasps in various degrees of flatness; a mouse, for God's sake, where did she find a mouse? Jumping on my back, she grabbed me round the neck.

'Get off it, no Daddy. It's mine.'

The pressure round my throat pushed the dust out in a huge spasm of coughing. As I tried to catch breath between wheezing and spluttering, she pulled the vanity case free and ran off downstairs.

I've been trying to work up the nerve to mention it since. The vanity case is nowhere to be seen. I don't want to upset her again. She didn't speak to me for the rest of yesterday. It makes me feel like I've violated her in some way. Despite the obvious health hazards of her little box full of fleas and maggot-riddled dead creatures, I know it's just her way of coping. She doesn't have much else. Her friends, like mine, have slowly vanished. Chloe's, because their parents think they're too young to have to talk about death – mine, because they're scared I do.

The *Shrek* video is on for the third time in twenty-four hours. It's the first and last film Trisha took Chloe to see. Chloe was only two at the time but supposedly there wasn't a peep out of her, aside from when they both sang along at the end. I couldn't join them as I was tutoring a client online that afternoon. I always have to leave the room before the karaoke scene at the end comes on as its glad-to-be-aliveness makes me wish I was dead.

As the final strains of 'Dance to the Music' fade out, I go back through. Chloe's not watching the screen. As my eyes adapt to the murky room, I realise she's staring at a money spider as it spins its way around her outstretched fingers. A chink of sunlight through the curtain catches the silky lustre. I notice her noticing me but she continues to gaze at her hand, holding it against the beam of light. I have a fleeting vision of us both being trapped under the fluff and the dust beneath the furniture: stifling; suffocating in dying light.

We need to get out. If we don't go out now I'm afraid we're never going to escape. I sit down on the settee beside her.

'You've made another new friend, then?'

'His name's Lilo. He lives behind the wall,' she beams at me, her anger from yesterday evaporated in an instant. We watch the tiny, black bug weave between her fingers until it spins its escape route, disappears down a silky thread and scurries off across the carpet.

'Bye bye, Lilo, we'll see you soon,' she waves after it. I wave too, to humour her, before broaching the subject of leaving the house.

First I suggest the zoo. There are lots of different kinds of animals there. But Chloe's teacher, Ms Gerard, has told her that zoos are cruel, apparently, and that the pupils should tell their parents they don't want to go there any more.

'. . . then it'll have to shut down and all the animals will get to go home and get set free.'

I try to tell her it's not that simple but she's adamant that Ms Gerard is right. She doesn't want to look at the sad animals. As I pull my hankie out of my pocket, I check how much cash I have left to do us 'til my cheque clears at midnight. I'm down to a few pound coins and loose change. I tell Chloe, Ms Gerard is probably right after all.

On the subject of the beach she's a little more enthusiastic but insists she'll only go if I let her go in for a swim. It's October, and the cold wind blowing in from the North Sea goes right through you, even walking along the sand fully clothed.

She suggests the baths, but there's people might be there I don't want to see. We compromise on the River Esk, to feed the ducks. More animals, unfortunately, but at least it gets us out of the bloody house.

We pop into the Italian shop on the High Street for an ice cream on the way. The girl who has a crush on me is serving. I'm not really in the mood.

'Hiya stranger. We thought you'd gone into hiding, eh, Marie?'

Marie who runs the shop comes over, with a look of well-used pity.

'Ah, wiv no seena ya down the Jaggy Thistle for a while. Yil need to come around one night,' she says in her Scottish/Italian lilt that I used to find so charming.

Mumbling something about being busy, I watch strawberry ice cream dribble down Chloe's chin onto her just-washed Adidas top, grab her cold, sticky hand and we leave.

I've got just enough money left for ten fags and the other ice cream I know Chloe will insist I buy her on the way back. There's plenty of food in the house, but I hate running out of money completely. It's only happened since Trisha died and makes me feel like I can't even manage basic things any more.

Chloe pulls me to a halt outside the Oxfam shop. She points at a tatty looking corn dolly, strung forlornly from a coat hanger in the window.

'It's a lucky dolly, Daddy. I saw it at school. The farmers use it to keep the animals from getting sick. Can I have it, Daddy? It's lucky. Please?'

There's three fags left in my old packet. If I get a packet of Rizla, I can make them last me the night. Figuring we both need a bit of luck, I succumb. Chloe is over the moon – sniffing it and lifting its straw arms up and down.

By the time we get along to the Esk, though, it's vanished – dropped in uninterest somewhere along the way. I get a sudden rush of rage, but subdue it into a quick, quiet sulk.

It must be the mallard mating season or something, as the ducks are all trying to mount each other. It's embarrassing. Despite this, they manage to demolish the stale French stick we brought in about thirty seconds flat. Then they're immediately jumping on each other's backs again. Chloe, no longer the centre of attention, goes into serious girning mode.

'This is rubbish. How could we not have just gone to the beach? I could swim in my t-shirt and pants. C'mon, dad . . . please?'

I try to distract her by pointing to a bluebottle on its

back, going down river, struggling to pull free of the gentle current. When she manages to focus on it, she erupts.

'You've got to save her, Dad. She's drowning. Come on,' she squeals, taking off down the riverbank after it. I follow her, flustered but grateful for this unexpected mutual pursuit. When she suddenly stops, I nearly fall over her.

'Aw Dad, she's stuck. You've got to save her.'

The insect has become lodged against a boulder. I'm not sure if it's the current spinning it round or it's still struggling for life. Chloe's picking up twigs and throwing them into the river, each one landing well short of the target. It's making her frantic.

I try throwing in a few sticks and pebbles but I'm equally hopeless, which just makes Chloe worse. I have to grab her hand to stop her launching herself into the Esk to rescue it.

A swan, tending her young, glides over to see what all the commotion is about. She seems to look at me, then Chloe, briefly scans the surface of the water and before we even have a chance to say goodbye, gulps down the unfortunate insect.

I anticipate Chloe's scream, but instead she starts beaming.

'Will that make baby swans now, Daddy? Will it come back as something else? See, we've seen it happen.'

I tell her, no, the swan just ate it for food, but it'll help the swan feed her own babies. She's immediately bawling and greeting again. Christ, what are you supposed to do? I have to restrain her from stoning the swan. A tattooed guy, fishing on the opposite bank, stands up, and shields his eyes to squint across at us as she screams in my arms. Typical. I give him the thumbs up and a look of long-suffering submission, which he probably can't see. He goes back to his fishing and his beer. He's too far away to tell whether his tan is that of someone foreign or your average Musselburgh waster. He looks blissfully unburdened by life either way – lucky bastard.

As I pull a grumbling Chloe away, salvation thankfully arrives again by way of an extremely overweight, slavery black Labrador, that comes bounding towards us and lunges at Chloe, tongue first. She's immediately all over it, kneeling down to make her face easier to lick. I let it lavish her with its foul, wet breath until its owner yells it back. Chloe's hand is dripping with doggy saliva but I don't make a fuss in case she starts up again.

We walk across the park towards the bowling green. None of my old Lodge seem to be about, so we sit on a bench. Chloe is unexpectedly fascinated by it all. Grabbing my arm, she gets me to explain what the people throwing the balls are trying to do and then whoops with delight every time someone takes a shot. Despite my reservations at having a six-year-old who's obsessed with road kill and the world's most boring sport, it's a relief to see her enthusiastic about something new.

The teams for the next game start to gather around us as the other game reaches the end. I feel someone squeezing my free arm. I turn to face Rachel, the wonderfully witty wife of my friend, Andrew. The lovely warm feeling her round, ruddy face gives me immediately chills when I realise she's in a wheelchair. I'd completely forgotten she'd been diagnosed with MS. It's so long since I've been in touch with them. She looks so genuinely pleased to see us both, I start to well up.

'When did you last have a day off, Nick? No offence, darlin', but you look awful . . .' she gives my arm another squeeze. 'Really, we'd love to look after Chloe if you fancy a bit of space. Even better, take him out my hair for a night.'

She grimaces at Andrew. He pulls a face back.

Chloe shuffles over, pretending to be shy.

'And you, look at you. You're all grown up. You going to keep your Auntie Rachel company for a while?'

Chloe squints at the wheelchair, fascinated.

'What's wrong with the lady, Daddy?'

'Chloe!' I say, embarrassed by her question and my inability to address it. Rachel laughs and asks her for a hug.

'Nothing having a chat with my favourite girl won't help.'

Andrew gestures towards the bar.

'Go on, Nick, go in and have a pint. She'll be fine with Rach. The boys have all been asking after you.'

The last thing I want to do is have to go over it all again with the guys from the Lodge.

'Honestly, I better be getting ba . . .'

'Nonsense, look at that pair. They're getting on like a house on fire. Get yourself in there and relax for a while.'

I look to Chloe for an escape, but she's completely caught up in Rachel explaining how the electronic wheelchair works. Going backwards and forwards in it. It's like I'm not even there. Andrew takes my arm and leads me towards the bar.

'Daddy be back soon. You look after Auntie Rachel.'

Chloe just grunts and carries on her crash course in disabled transport mechanics.

Andrew pushes me through the door of the bar and waves me off.

'They can watch me play bowls together. I'll show her how it's really done.'

The last game has ended. I stand in the doorway till the team coming off goes into the bar, then I hide behind them. I don't want any of the boys to see me. I can't even afford a bloody half pint, and I've now only got two fags left to last me 'til morning.

I walk loudly across the bar towards the toilets, nearly bumping straight into Peter McVeigh and Larry Marshall standing, engrossed, by the fruit machine. In a panic, I rush out the other exit into the street.

God, this is pathetic.

At the corner, I cross back over onto the park. The black

Labrador is now chasing a ball with a collie, as the owners, a man and a woman, stand talking. I wonder if theirs is a planned or chance meeting. Another expensively grungy looking couple are pulling a graffiti patterned kite across the sky, giggling over who gets to guide it. I try to think about Trisha and me walking across here onto the beach in the early days, before Chloe, but all I can see is the cold, ivory shell she turned into the second after she let out her last breath; the brown brain drool that came down the tube from her nose; the absolute indignity of it.

A cold wave of nausea flushes over me and I think I'm going to pass out. I hobble over to the park toilets.

Squeaking the heavy door open, I feel immediately better, being back in an enclosed space; the buzz of the ventilator; the smell of disinfectant. The place is pristine – clean trays with fresh soap; real linen dispensers, a vase of flowers. It hardly even smells of piss.

There's a guy already standing at the urinals, but I have trouble pissing in public so I go into one of the two cubicles. I sit down to pee, just wanting a moment to myself; somewhere quiet. I hear the guy at the urinal cough, spit and leave. Hugging myself, I savour the feeling of release, alone in this tiny space. I never even have peace in the bathroom at home. Chloe's always knocking on the door, wanting a sandwich; wanting to watch a video; wanting every bit of me for herself.

I look around the cubicle. The high standards of hygiene

and decor aren't quite so apparent in here. There's some half arsed scrawlings on the back of the door, but nothing interesting or readable. There are brown marks against the tiles where fags have been stubbed out. The toilet roll holder has been pulled off the wall, leaving a hole in the partition.

Instinctively, I peer through.

I just see the tattoos at first, jumping up and down like an animated film. A once only, exclusive viewing. Imagining the tanned man on the other side of the river, a ball of fire ignites in my belly. Slowly leaning back from the hole, I try to see the rest, as I gently rub my pain, trying to look away, staring at the floor but the image is set in my mind like a just-switched-off television screen. I have to look again.

A big brown eye is looking back and then is gone. In an instant I know I'm caught. I can't catch my breath. I'm terrified but still desperate for relief. I want to destroy the evidence but it won't go away. I can see the side of his training shoe, protruding through from the next cubicle. It just makes me worse. I want to look through the hole again, just to see what's happening, but I don't want the guy to think I was wanking over him because I wasn't, I really wasn't.

The partition reverberates, as if he's fallen against it. As I stare at my cock, willing it to empty, he stuffs his cock through the hole. I'm immediately on my knees, my right leg squashed in abstract round the base of the toilet, the underside of the pan digging into my back. I can't get enough of him in my mouth. My neck feels like it's about to snap but I suck greedily and hopelessly, my hand twisted but still beating between my legs. As he cums down my throat, I release onto the cool nylon of the lining of my jacket. Woozy from release, I'm still drying him with my tongue when I hear the main toilet door squeak open and Chloe's voice shout through,

'Daddy, are you there, Daddy? We're looking for you.'

'Eh . . . ok sweetheart . . . I'll be out in a minute,' I stammer, as his cock disappears again.

'Hurry Dad, Auntie Rachel has to go and I've something to show you, c'mon.'

She mumbles something and I hear the door squeak shut again.

My leg has seized up against the base of the toilet. As I try to free my foot from behind the cistern, I feel a twinge in my already aching back but my fear and sense of responsibility are still dissolved in adrenaline. Standing up, there's no toilet paper. I wipe the mess with a long-dud lottery ticket and a few old bus tickets. I feel overjoyed.

Checking my jacket in the mirror by the sink, most of the wet bits are inside. Smoothing down my hair, I leave.

Chloe immediately grabs my hand and pulls me towards the beach. I wave apologetically to Rachel and Andrew as he wheels her back towards the bowling club. Chloe huffs and puffs at my slow, stiff progress.

'Och, Dad, c'mon. See what I've found.'

Then the pair of us are kneeling on the sand, staring

intently at something. A dead starling. Chloe pulls me closer.

'Please dad, just this last one. Please. Just let me keep it until it changes. Please . . .'

I glance back across the park as the tattooed man from the river disappears up toward the High Street. I put the dead bird in my pocket.

We go for another ice cream on the way home.

The Bez

IT'S SCORCHING. A million Highland midges are trying to bite me to death and it's like cycling the Tour de France in the wrong direction. Honest, I've nearly been knocked into the canal about twenty times by ugly families and weedy guys in Lycra coming the other way. They don't even ring their bells. Plus, I thought this was meant to be a cold country? It feels like I've sweated all the fluid out of my body. I never sweated at all till we moved to this bumhole of a place. It's probably to do with that nuclear power station we passed on the way up in the train.

There's thousands of ducks and swans in the shade by the bridge. I stop for a rest. Leaning my bike against the wall, I sit on the grass and pick a scab I've been saving on my elbow. I wonder if they get snakes around here. Who knows what deformed creature might crawl out and poison me? A man-pigeon chases a lady-pigeon along the path, trying to jump on her back. His chest is puffed out like he thinks he's some sort of sex god. I chew the crusty bits round the edges of my scab as I watch them. I like pigeons. They don't care what anyone thinks.

A trundling sound is getting closer. A clunkety-clunk echoes inside the bridge. Then there's a big cloud of dust and this boy's in front of me. He's about my age, eleven, maybe a bit older. I've seen him before but I don't know him. He runs on to catch his skateboard then walks back to my bike. Great. I've only been sitting here about a minute and someone's going to steal my bike. He crouches down and examines it – squeezing the tyres, trying the brakes, running his hand over the saddle. Is he checking it's good enough to nick? He dings the bell.

'A Tacana, pure boss!'

Does he mean it's crap? Cheeky get thinks my bike's crap.

'It's my dad's. I'm just using it while mine gets more gears put on.'

Can bikes get more gears? I'm so shocked someone's talking to me I'm saying anything.

'Solid,' he says, stroking the handlebars like he's in love with it. Getting on, he tries to pedal with half his weight against the wall. He wobbles around, looking stupid, but he doesn't seem bothered. I sort of like him. I've seen him skateboarding on the hill across from our house. I remember his shirt – black with flames coming up from the bottom. It sort of makes him stick out.

'Your shirt's cool.'

Great, he'll think I'm a homo now. He struggles off the bike and struts about.

'It's boss, eh? My dad supplies markets. He gets gear all over, like. Stuff they won't get here for years.'

He's puffing up like the pigeon, looking really proud.

'You want one? I can get you one no bother.'

'Yeah? I can get money off Mum. How much are they?'

He looks at me like I'm a spazoid.

'No sweat, big man.'

He sits down beside me. I suddenly notice the stink of dog shit around us. The sun must be making it melt. He better not think it's me. But he's smoking and staring across at the canal. He takes a big drag and hands me it.

'There you go, pal.'

The smell coming off it takes my mind off the dog shit. It smells like our old house when Mum used to have her dinner parties. She used to say it was Sophie's menthols, but this is exactly what it smelt like. Mum is such a liar. The one he's passed me is tiny – about the size of a match. Like the ones they smoke in American films. Much cooler than Mum's pretend fags.

'Go on. It's legal.'

I give it a couple of sucks and hold the smoke in my mouth. He's staring at the canal again, which is good as I'm probably doing it wrong. My cheeks start hurting from holding it in, so I blow it out in a big ball. I hope I don't start laughing like a mong.

'See the ducks? The white ones? Know why they're like that? What makes them white?'

Handing him it back, I go over to the bank for a look. There's about a hundred mucky brown ducks but only two white ones. They've got bright yellow beaks like they're out of a cartoon. I don't want to try and guess and make a twat of myself.

He comes over and stands beside me. I stand half off the bank, leaning forward as far as I can without falling in. He laughs and copies me. We try and lean further and further than each other till I slip forward too far and he grabs me just in time. It feels cool. Like he's saved me. He looks sort of embarrassed though and goes back over to my bike. Kneeling down, he runs his hands across the tyres. I think he must have a pervy thing about stroking bikes.

'So what are your new gears? I thought twenty-seven was the most you could get on these.'

Bugger, I don't know about stuff like that. I only said it was Dad's cos I thought it might stop him stealing it.

'Er . . . just the same . . . but better ones . . . sort of.'

He knows I'm lying but he just says, 'Boss,' again and carries on feeling it up.

'I had a Tamarak, when we lived in Ireland.'

'IRELAND!' I say all loud, like a twat. Luckily he keeps on talking.

'It was well cool. I could cycle along the seafront all the way into town. If it was really sunny, I could see America.'

A map of the world comes into my head. I think of the size of the Atlantic, between Ireland and New York. I know all about it because I used to stare at it in the atlas all the time. It took Dad nearly eight hours to get there when he flew from Heathrow. Eight hours. It's the second biggest ocean in the world.

'You can't see that far, can you? It's absolutely gigantic. And it's curved, so it'd be over the other side, wouldn't it?'

He just stares at me.

'Have you been there, like?'

'My dad's been to New York.'

'Ooh!' He yanks the bike away from the wall. 'Well I'm just telling you what I saw every day. I don't know about curves and stuff. Maybe you just can't see from the American side.'

Why did I mention it? Climbing onto my bike, he rests his skateboard on the handlebars. He's going to go away now. I don't care about the bike. I just sort of want him to stay.

'C'mon, I'll give you a backie along the path,' he says.

I'm so pleased I get this stupid big grin on my face. I get on the back, so he doesn't notice. It almost looks like there's a light shining out from his shirt – like the flames are real. If I mention this he will think I'm a tit, though, so I keep my idiot mouth shut this time.

It's a disaster. We're wobbling about, swaying all over the place. The skateboard keeps nearly falling off and I have to keep grabbing onto him. It's sort of fun but I can't relax cos I'm scared I'm going to tear his brilliant shirt. I feel a mobile in his pocket while I'm trying to hang on. Maybe we can text each other.

We skid to a stop where the path leads onto the street. I jump off, out of breath and really hot again from the strain of trying to stay on. The ducks are all down this end now. They must have followed us. The white ones are washing their faces in the water.

'So why are they like that again?'

He does a wheelie.

'Did your round-the-world daddy never tell you, like?'

I shrug. He cycles up close to me and whispers,

'The seagulls rape their mammies.'

I think he's joking but I can tell straightaway from his face, it's true.

'Serious, my uncle showed me. They wait till one's on its own then they attack. The noise the ducks make when they're doing it, it's horrible, like.'

He flaps his arms and squawks really loudly. The ducks all speed off in the other direction again.

No wonder the brown ones go round in big groups. The white ones' beaks are the same colour as seagulls as well. It's so obvious. God – seagulls, pigeons, they're all at it.

'D'you think all birds are sex mad?'

'They are once they've met me!' he shouts, doing another wheelie. I smile and pretend that's what I meant. God, I bet he's had loads of girlfriends. It's always guys that don't seem bothered that girls seem to go for. Maybe he's got a few going spare.

He starts walking my bike towards the top of the street.

'C'mon, this is boring. We'll go and play snooker?'

I'm meant to be at Grandma's. As if Mum's going to find out if I don't go though. They only speak to each other about once every hundred years.

'C'mon. My uncle runs the club down the road. We'll get crisps and juice.'

He starts making squawking noises again.

'Hurry, here's the seagulls. They shag posh boys too . . . quick.'

I jump back on. The street's dead busy but I want to stay with him. I'm scared he'll disappear if he goes away now.

He lets go the brakes and we take off down the hill. I'd never realised how steep it was before. We're absolutely speeding. A car comes out the side road and has to swerve to avoid us. We just skid round and keep going. My nerves have gone. It's like we're flying.

'*Bez draws up close to Schumacher. He accelerates. Schumacher struggles to regain control as Bez dashes past into second. There's only Coulthard to deal with now. Coulthard's slowing. He can't take the pace. He's pulling into the pit. IT'S ALL OVER FOR COULTHARD!!*'

This is so fantastic. Bez – what a completely cool name.

We race down the street, straight through the red lights at the bottom and round onto the main road. A bus horn honks at about a thousand decibels as we miss going under it by about a millimetre. It's amazing. It feels like we're immortal.

'*As Bez crosses the finishing line, the crowd erupt. They have their new champion . . . and what a champion he is.*'

We pull into a side street. I didn't want us to stop. Not ever. The blood's beating through my body really fast. Even my sweat feels good. Sort of clean.

Bez tells me to get off and hands me the skateboard. Lifting the bike onto his shoulder, he walks up to a big door and pushes an intercom.

'Open up, it's The Bez!'

Is this it? I never knew this was a snooker hall. There's no sign outside. It just looks like an office or something. As we push in and walk up the steps, I feel really excited but try to act like I do stuff like this all the time.

When I open the door at the top though, it feels like we've just walked into an explosion. A burst of sweaty heat, booming music, yelling and swearing blasts us in the face. We walk into a hot, sticky, stinky, smoky room. It's totally disgusting. Like the smell when you pass a homeless person but about a billion times worse.

There's hundreds of drunken, skanky grown-ups playing pool, playing darts, arguing, singing football songs, standing round fruit machines. Bez walks straight up to the bar, like he hasn't even noticed them. I have to push past the mingers to keep up.

'Feel my cheeks, Kath. I just cycled five miles with posh boy there on the back.'

Kath must work here. She's in her twenties or something but is still pretty and sort of happy looking. She smiles across at me, then gives the bike a worried look.

'Aw, Ben!'

Bez starts putting it behind the bar.

'Naw Kath, it's his, honest. Go and watch it while we have a game? Please?'

She shakes her head and does her nice smile again. Her blouse has flames on it like Bez's shirt, except hers is tight. It looks cool on her too, even though she's old. She puts the bike in the corner and a tin of Irn Bru on the bar.

'What's your pal want? You got a name, pet? He's no manners.'

'Give him a pint,' growls an old guy with a giant raspberry nose.

'Chuck in a few pies an' all. Look at the state of him,' yells a flaky-tanned fat toad beside him.

I say my name and ask for the same as Bez but my voice comes out in a tiny squeak. I'm amazed when she puts another tin on the bar and says, 'There you go, Pete.' She must have satellite ears. My thank you is drowned out by a group of pensioners moaning for more drink but she hopefully hears me anyway.

It's a relief to go through to the actual snooker hall, away from the sweaty twats. It's not like I expect. There are about twenty tables in the same giant room. Only one is being used, by a skinny bloke and an enormous fat woman dressed like a man. It's dark and quiet and much cooler. I can still see the drunk people through the glass but it's separate and I feel a hundred times safer.

The light over the back table flickers on as Bez walks over with the balls. He's set them up before he asks if I can actually play.

'Dad tried to teach me a few times. Before we moved.'

I wish. If they hadn't sent me off to boarding school, I guess he might have. That's where I really learned to play snooker but I'm not mentioning that to Bez. He already thinks I'm posh enough as it is.

'First frame!' he shouts, breaking loudly, knocking reds everywhere and a fluke one into the middle. I tap the table like they do at the Crucible when the other player does a good shot. Jammy shit.

Next go, though, the blue hits the edge of the pocket and misses. Bez does a huge fart. It's so strong, it makes our eyes water, so we both end up missing a few. Honestly, the smell lasts for ages. It's like a chemical weapon. I'd do a revenge one but we laugh so much at his, I need the toilet.

He misses another easy one. It leaves me on a shot I used to practise all the time at school – red along the bottom cushion into the corner.

'Watch this. It's a classic. Steve Davis used to do it.'

I'm concentrating so much, my tongue's sticking out but it misses by a mile. Bez starts killing himself.

'Yeah, classic. Is that why he doesn't play any more?'

I feel my face going red so I go over to open my juice. The fat woman's going out to the bar. When she opens the partition door, a group of pissheads burst into, 'Who Let the Dogs Out?' I hate that song. A girl I liked back home used to make her pals sing it when I went past. Every time I hear it now it makes me feel glad her mum died.

'C'mon? I'll foul you for time wasting. Give's another Steve Davis special.'

It's almost like a miracle. I get a five ball break – three reds and two browns. None of them are easy. It was probably thinking about Claire made me angry.

'COME ON STEVE DAVIS, COME ON STEVE DAVIS!' I sing. I'm not usually like this but the good break just makes me feel really confident.

'Keep it down a bit, eh? This isnae a fucking playground,' yells the skinny bloke on the other table.

What a cheek. We were hardly making any noise. I feel like yelling back at the miserable sod.

'C'mon. He's just trying to be macho cos Vanessa's back,' says Bez as the fat woman flubbers down to take a shot. Her cue skids over the white, missing it completely. She turns round and makes a big elephant noise at us, like it's our fault she's complete crap. It's so pathetic it's hilarious. Bez and me laugh our heads off, half cos it's funny and half to annoy them even more.

I collapse over the end of our table, pretending to be her having a heart attack. Bez tries to ignore me but still misses his next shot. Lucky get still nearly snookers me though.

'Another stunning safety from this young man,' he says in his presenter voice, clapping himself.

I twirl my cue like Tom Cruise did in that old film, then try a pool shot. The red bounces off the cushion, straight into the opposite bag. I dance round in a circle with the cue above my head. Bez does a serious face.

'I'm sorry but I'll have to foul you for celebrating too much. This isn't a fucking playground, you know.'

Pulling my t-shirt over my head, I give him the V-sign. When I take it off, he's pretending to change the scoreboard.

'Davis, foul. The Bez, four points.'

Twirling my cue again, I go for blue into the middle, then red into top, then down for re-spotted blue back into middle. Bez whispers,

'And the crowd hold their breath as this remarkable old boy goes for gold.'

It makes me mishit, but the red comes off the cushion and spins down brilliantly into the corner. I do the commentary this time, Superbowl style –

'Without even touching the sides. How about that boy!'

Bez looks stunned.

'Pure amazing! Come up every day. I'm always here over

the holidays. D'you want to? You won't have to pay if you ask for me.'

How good is today? And now I can have another four weeks of it before I have to start my new school. I think about Bez on his skateboard across from my house and wonder if we were supposed to meet. I'm sure he was playing over there the day we moved in.

As I bend over to take the blue, there's suddenly this giant bang, like something's collapsed outside. By the time I look round it's like America's invaded the bar. Everyone seems to be fighting. Fists and bottles and people are flying everywhere. Because we're in the dark, watching it through the glass though, it's like it's on a giant screen. Even the fatgirlslim couple are gawping at it. Skeletor's not complaining about the noise now, though. Bez gulps his juice like nothing's happening.

'It's just my uncle cracking up. They had a fight at the golf. Just ignore it.'

But it's getting worse. I see the old raspberry-nose man getting smacked round the head. There's a young guy standing on the seats, Jackie Chan-ing three skinheads away with the heavy end of a cue. A group of men are holding someone over the pool table while they punch him. It's like the WWF except with real people.

'Christ Bez, look at the blood on that bloke's head!'

He's still waiting for me to take my next shot.

'Yeah, that's my uncle. C'mon. If you don't look, you

can't give evidence. Just play,' he says, like I'm starting to get on his nerves.

The glass partition keeps rattling as people get pushed against it. Someone's going to come smashing through any second. Fatso's trying to get past Skeletor for a better look but he's holding her back.

'He should let her go. She could flatten them all to death.'

We start laughing again. It wasn't even that funny but it just sort of feels safer when we're laughing. Bez is probably right. If we pretend not to notice, no-one's going to bother us. He must know it's ok. Nobody's going to hit two kids, surely. I go over to take my shot.

'A tsunami couldn't break this man's cool as he bends down for his next safety.'

I put in a brilliant long red. It helps my panicky feeling but I really need the loo.

'Is there a toilet through here? I'm dying for a pee.'

Bez points out at the battlefield and offers me his empty tin.

'Use that if you're really desperate. I'll put it out there when it calms down. Hopefully one of them'll drink it.'

I grab it without thinking. It's a bit disgusting but I'll never hold out till the war outside ends.

'Dear me. Davis' safety play has fallen apart. He's pissing in a tin. Dear oh dear. It almost seems like the Hurricane's back,' he giggles as I run around looking for a dark bit. I go behind

one of the side tables, put my back to everything and try to pee into the can. Nothing happens. It's pitch black but I still feel like everybody's looking at me. I try to pretend I'm in the bathroom at home, with the tap running but it's no good. What a twat I am.

The partition door bangs open and I hear someone running into the hall. I don't want them to catch me standing in the dark with my knob in my hand, so I zip back up. When I get back over to our table, there's a bloke in an Arsenal top crouching behind it, with his head split open. Bez is trying to talk to him but the man's so scared, he doesn't seem to hear. It makes me scared. It's not just the blood and the gash in his head. I've just never seen an adult look so terrified before.

He peers over the edge of the table, eyes bulging, watching for whoever's after him. He's trembling so much, it's like he's having a fit. His face is white, and there's sweat running into the blood, making it drip off his chin. Even though I'm shitting it myself, I can't stop staring at him. I've never seen someone injured in real life before. It's sort of fascinating.

'Is there another way out of here?' he asks in a shaky whisper, keeping his eye on the door. Bez is watching it too now. Even he's starting to look worried. It makes me feel really frightened.

'Just stay with us, pal. Wait till it's over. You'll be ok.'

Aw Bezzy! What's he saying? It's not our problem. Why can't we go hide under a table and leave him? He must have done something bad if someone's that angry with him. Everything's just going horrible. I'll get stabbed and Mum'll find out I was lying. She'll kill me for coming to a place like this. I'll have to say I got mugged, if I've not already been murdered.

The scared man stands up. Maybe he's come to his senses and realised innocent kids could get hurt because of him. I pray he's going to make a run for it. Instead, he grabs my cue off the table and starts swinging it in front of him like a light sabre. Worse still, Bez goes and stands in front of him, blocking his way.

'Look pal, just put that down, eh? I can't let you go out there.'

The scared man's stopped again. It's like he can't work up the nerve to go out but is too embarrassed to hide again. Why doesn't Bez just leave him? Instead, he makes a swipe for the cue. The scared man yanks it away and lifts it above his head, like he's going to whack Bez. Please no.

My body freezes and everything suddenly seems to go into weird, slow motion. I see Bez take a few steps backwards, pull something out of his pocket and point it at the man. My legs give way. As I hit the floor, the cue clatters down in front of me. I think it's coming for my head and burst out crying. I can't help it. It's like I can't hold in the scaredness any more. I wrap my arms over my skull, waiting to be hit.

I realise my trackie-bottoms are soaking. I've wet myself

and I can't even remember. I hate him for getting me like this. I hate him and his scummy uncle and all his skanky friends. I hate his shirt and his stupid voices. I can't let him see I've pissed myself. I hate him.

I jump up and run down the hall, away from them. Yanking open the door, I push my way through the horrible, fighting drunks, the bloody heads and all the other smelly, disgusting people in this scummy, stinking place. They're even fighting on the stairway. I dash past them and pull open the heavy door at the bottom. I hate him. He can keep my bike. I never want to have to see him again. I'm out on the busy main road again. I limp back along it in my heavy, wet jogging bottoms, feeling sick, crying for my daddy and home.

There is a Light that Never Goes Out

THEY TOOK MY bag with all my things and now I'm stranded. I had to run away so I've no idea where I am. It's a busy road with four lanes of traffic. Does that make it a motorway? There are fields on this side and a high wall on the other. I passed a sign a while back that said Edinburgh, so I think I'm going the right way.

There's faint flickering to my left but it could be miles in the distance. I reach a small lane turning off towards the flickering. It's better I keep to the main road though. I stand waiting to cross. The traffic all seems to be going straight past, but if a car suddenly turns when I'm half way over, I've had it. I decide to walk down the lane to find a safer bit.

Straightaway, I notice a light, just on its own, not far from where I am. There's movement in the light – like flames. As I pull away from the noise of the main road, I can make out a different kind of sound – a human sound.

Like someone coughing. Walking towards it, into the darkness, there's a figure hunched over, retching onto the grass. He is silhouetted by the light I thought was a fire but I realise is a car parked in a lay-by. The light is on because the door's open. There are several people inside. I can hear laughing. Men laughing. It's a happy sound so I keep going towards it. As I draw level with the vomiting person, I touch his shoulder. A boy bolts upright and lets out a squeal.

'What the fu . . . !'

Steadying himself, he tries to focus on me, and then darts off towards the car, wailing. The door slams and there's a commotion inside. I look behind me but there's just blackness. I can still hear the traffic but I've walked down further than I thought. I take fright. What if it's them? Turning round to make for the road, I trip into a trough in the grass. One of my shoes comes off. As I bend down to find it, I see the car backing up the road. It is them.

I have one more fumble then give up and start running towards the traffic sound, with the car backing up behind me. Even before they overtake and drive in front to block my path, I know I'm not going to make it. If I can just keep calm; not get too emotional; take a step back.

The window rolls down and a dimply-faced boy smiles out in a puff of smoke.

'You all right, sweetheart? A bit lost, eh?'

Smiling back seems like the best idea.

'I was just trying to cross the road. I didn't mean to scare your friend.'

There's great hilarity from the smoky car. The dimpled boy grins.

'Sorry doll, he's paranoid enough as it is. Anyway, you all right? You want a lift somewhere?' He roars the engine. 'I'm the fastest taxi in the West.'

'Just as soon as he gets his own motor,' shouts a voice from behind the steamed up windows.

I'm smiling. It's not them. They're far too young.

'I'm ok, thanks. I don't live far. Thanks anyway.'

'Sure? I'll have you wherever you're going in five minutes. No charge for pretty young ladies.'

Another boom of laughter from inside, plus a few wolf whistles. It makes me feel good.

'Thanks again, but I'm fine. Good luck with the taxis though.'

He has a lovely face. He watches me cross the road, then blows me a kiss as they take off back into the darkness.

I think about his face as I walk back towards the road. Imagine he is holding my hand, pulling me gently towards home. It was a mischievous, happy face. I feel ten times stronger having met him.

I'm back on the main road in no time. The pavement chills my shoeless foot but I stride with a new confidence. The noisy whiz of speeding traffic is invigorating. I imagine I'm striding through Colinton Dell with Robert. We've just made love against the giant oak, near where the rabbits all sit in the dark then disappear in a massive black wave when they hear us coming. We're late and he is rushing back home, but I know I can now go out with my friends and update them on our daring, wonderful affair. It was the perfect arrangement. Nowadays I've got him all to myself.

It starts to rain – not heavy – just that warm drizzle one notch up from mist. It settles on my face and hair and hands and makes me feel clean. I stick out my tongue to taste it. It tastes of health and life and petrol. I walk with conviction.

They took my bag with all my numbers and tickets and money and make-up and keys in it but they didn't hurt me, did they? Again, I try to remember what happened but all I can see are the dimples on that boy's face. It's happened before. I've been so frightened my mind won't let me remember for ages afterwards. Who cares? Those dimples. You pretty young lady. Am I near home? Will he pass again? I'll remember his face forever.

I'm coming up to another sign – Edinburgh City Centre – Leith. I am come home, I say to myself, just like Bonnie Prince Charlie once did, in a rowing boat with Flora MacDonald in a matching dress. Someone showed me it in a book, once. Probably Robert. He's always showing me things and trying to make me talk about stuff on the news I know nothing about.

Then I notice the red light on the top of Corstorphine

Hill to my left and realise I must be out near the airport. I'm both pleased and shocked by this realisation. What the heck am I doing out here?

I'm aware of the sound of a car drawing up beside me, conspicuously slow on the fast road. Sure that the boy with the dimples has come back for me, I turn around with the smile I've been practising. There is a thickset man with glasses sitting in the driver's seat. He looks sad. The window opens. This time no smoke, just a strong scent of cream soda like the ice cream parlour I used to sit in with my dinner money. He glowers at me like I should know who he is.

'You look lost. Do you want a lift?'

I squint through the open window. His face looks vaguely familiar – like someone from a television programme I watch when I'm not really watching. I'm sure he lives in our street.

'C'mon, get in. It's raining.'

I want to explain that it's not real rain. It's rain that cleanses you and makes you feel like a baby. Who is he, again? He's not one of them because he's wearing a uniform. Not a soldier. Something cheap looking.

It is getting heavier now. I never really notice my neighbours. I must know him. I better get back and start thinking of excuses to tell Robert. I'll tell him I left my bag somewhere. He'll go berserk if I tell him I was robbed. He'll think I invited it. I can't remember what happened. It'll make him go mad.

The man is out beside me, opening the passenger door, ushering me in.

'C'mon, it's making the car cold. Get in.'

The rain is deepening. The cold car seems a better option than walking down this road getting even more soaked.

'Look, will you get in?'

I stand in a puddle on the way but luckily it's my shoeless foot, so I don't ruin another pair. How the hell am I going to explain that to Robert? Maybe he'll already be in bed. What time is it? I've no idea what time it is. They must have my watch as well. How can I make an excuse for where I've been when I don't even know what time it is? It feels good to sit down. The car isn't cold at all.

Once he shuts the car door, it's even warmer. I could sleep. I just want to snuggle up to Robert and go to sleep. I'm dying to see him. Even if he is angry with me – it's never for long. He gets it out of his system then we're fine. The other door slams.

'What street you in again?'

I tell him my address. Why didn't I just let these boys take me in the first place? I can't remember why I didn't want to get right home but I'm glad I'm going there now. I watch my mystery man as he drives. His eyes are tiny and bat-like from the side of his thick glasses. He doesn't talk. I expect him to say something but he doesn't. Probably best that way, since I can't remember much about either him or what happened.

Outside the window is getting more familiar – I'm getting closer to home – the zoo, the Posthouse Hotel where we had Christmas Dinner last year. I know where I am now. Then he takes a turning in the wrong direction, up towards Slateford.

'Sorry, it's the other way. It's Balgreen.'

He loses his rag.

'Shut your fucking mouth. I need to go somewhere first, ok?'

I shut up and switch off. It always makes me switch off, when people shout and swear. I just let him drive. At least I know where I am now. We're driving up towards the slaughterhouse. The field in front is empty. They must have killed all the sheep today. You can still smell the manure.

He parks up the side. I expect him to get out, but he starts fiddling with the radio.

'What d'you want to listen to? Classical?'

I like classical. I like allsorts.

'I don't mind. Can I go home soon though? I need to get chips.'

I've worked out I'm four chip shops from home. I'm starving. If I got out now I could eat mine going down the road then get Robert a supper. Say I had to wait. Then I remember I've no money.

He takes my hand and puts it on the radio and tells me to tune in to something I like. It feels like there's suddenly a lot less space in the car. I don't want to listen to anything. They took all my money. I feel like everything suddenly depends on me making it to the chip shop.

Taking my hand off the radio, he pushes it towards his lap. Oh dear. This is different now. He squeezes my fingers round his thing and makes me rub. This is different. I'm watching what my hand is doing, and thinking it looks strangely nice, but I'm scared. Sad for Robert even if he never finds out. He squeezes my fingers painfully and makes me rub really quickly. It's an awkward angle and there's a pain in my shoulder but I just want it to be over.

As he tries to push my face down towards it, it shudders and explodes over my hand and his trousers. He doesn't make any noise. Just lets out a silent sigh. I sort of like it but too much has already happened. I'll go back and blurt something out now. I touch it on his trousers. It is warm. I taste it. I've not tasted it for a long time. It makes me smile and want a man inside me again.

I suddenly, more than anything, want this man to hold me and kiss me and suck on my breasts and put his fingers inside me. But he starts up the car and pulls out back round the stinky field.

'Where d'you stay again?'

Snowdrops start falling on the windscreen, turned neon green by the traffic lights. It's quite romantic.

'Across from the library. Just by the park'll be fine. This has to be our little secret, though, ok?'

He stares at me hard.

'I'll put you out here, you dirty old slag! Don't threaten me. Don't fucking try to threaten me,' he growls.

My mouth tastes sour. I feel ashamed. I wipe his mess off my hand onto the seat.

'Just at the park, please.'

I've switched off again and stare out the window at the things I usually miss when I'm on the bus. The church is now flats. The swing park is now a car park. It's cold in the car now. Cold like a fish. How could I?

We drive past the Water of Leith. I feel a sort of chilled elation at being so close to home now. I'll pretend to fall straight asleep when I get in so I don't have to try and explain. Robert likes it best when he thinks I'm asleep. I can tell by the things he comes out with. I'll pretend to be sleeping. It will be lovely just to be close to him.

He stops at the entrance to the park.

'Right, get out. This'll do you.'

I look across the road. The chip shop opposite is still open. It has new lights. I remember I have to get Robert's supper. I look at the man. He's sitting all solid, waiting for me to go. It annoys me.

'I need to get chips. I've no money. I got mugged earlier.'

Looking at me like I'm dirt, he fishes in his back pocket. He hands me a fiver, leans over me, and opens the door.

'Now fuck off – you old boot!'

I take the money and leave my surviving shoe in his car

to even myself up. He screeches off towards the town as I cross the road to the shop.

Joe and Ella aren't working tonight. There's two younger boys – one handsome in an acne-scarred way, the other fat and greasy like a big chip. I can feel them sizing me up as I study the strangely shaped deep fried things. Then they both start laughing – looking straight at me and laughing like they know what I've just done. I make for the door in a panic. When I try to push it open, though, I just bang against it. They've locked it somehow from behind the counter.

'Pull!' one of them shouts, still howling with laughter.

It confuses me, then I realise he means the door. I yank it open. It's heavier than I expect and I get a sharp pain in my shoulder. I let out a yelp, which just makes them laugh all the more.

I rush down the street, trying not to cry. My bare feet splash on the cold, wet pavement. My feet are filthy and there's mud up my ankles. I've still no idea what I'm going to tell Robert. There's so much to explain but too many gaps I can't fill. He's going to explode. Crumpling the five pound note in my hand, I throw it into a garden I pass. It's one less thing to explain.

There's dozens of cars parked sideways on both sides of our street. There must be something on at Murrayfield. I'll say I got caught up in the crowd. Someone in the crowd stole my bag. I was trying to find it. Oh no. I'll have to ring the bell. He'll be so annoyed. It looks like every light in the house is on. It's ridiculous. What's he playing at?

The streetlights seem stronger than usual as well. He'll notice the dirt on my legs before I'm even in the door. The television is booming in the front room. Everything seems louder and brighter.

There's movement through the glass panel then the door's opened by an unshaven man in a filthy t-shirt.

'Oh God . . . Sharleen!' he screams into the house. I try to see behind him.

'What's going on? What are you doing in my house? Where's my husband?'

He tries to keep me at the door, and shouts for Sharleen again. The hall is a different colour. The lampshades have been changed. I look at the door again. 27. It's my door. This is our house.

An equally scruffy woman pushes past him and scowls at me.

'Oh Jesus, you can't keep doing this. I've got two infants and you're starting to scare them.'

I'm crying. I just want Robert to come out and tell me what's going on.

'Please. I don't know what you're doing in my house, but please can I see my husband? Please.'

She gestures the man to go back in the house. They're going to get him. It's ok. She takes a step towards me and holds out her hand.

'Look, we can't go on like this. The police'll take you back. Jeff'll phone the home to let them know you're here. Don't you remember?'

It's wet. I don't remember. I don't remember anything any more apart from green snowdrops, baby rain and a lovely face with dimples.

This is My Story, This is My Song

'. . . *HE WAS MEANT to meet us at the snooker club. We were waiting in the bar when I got the call. The cunt doing sixty in the Range Rover landed in a field with whiplash and a dislocated wrist. He phoned the ambulance. His mobile was still fucking working, can you believe that? Ronnie's van spun over three times then smashed face down on a wall. He had no chance.'*

I read Ian's email for about the tenth time, but still it seems like a newspaper story you'd see about some stranger.

The driving was Ronnie's first real work since the engineering plant burnt down, taking with it his job, pension and savings he'd been encouraged to invest in the company's shares. I try to work out where Granton and the shell of the plant should be, as my plane drops over the Forth. The surge of pride I always feel when I fly over the bridges overtakes me, though. I think it's called coming home.

I grab a taxi rather than wait ten minutes for the airport

bus. It's already half-nine and we're leaving for Mortonhall about eleven. They'll all have been in the pub since it opened. Not that I want to get pissed. I just need a few swifties to help me deal with the fact that Ronnie won't be there. Not today, not ever.

By Ingliston, I'm getting really maudlin, thinking about the last time I spoke to him. He phoned about hospitality tickets for the Hearts/Celtic game I couldn't make it up for. I said they must have got lost in the post. They're still sitting on top of my fridge. I just never bothered my arse.

I phone Steph on the mobile to cheer myself up. She's on her way out to Chalk Farm to buy more useless shite to clutter our flat. She's snappy because she hates me coming up for the home games, and thinks my best pal's funeral is some added sort of drunken conspiracy.

'So why didn't you phone me last time you were there? Why switch your mobile off?'

I get this one every couple of days. It's a cardinal sin. Thirty-six hours a month, I come up here, go see the football, kick a ball about for two hours, then fly down again. She tells me not to bother coming back. This time it's really over. As I'm already in Russell Road, this sounds fine so I hang up, and switch off the phone.

Ian's outside the pub as we pull up. He's gabbing into his mobile, swaggering about, dead cocky, doesn't notice me paying the driver. I slam the taxi door.

'Hey cunt, want some?'

He turns around with his magic big grin.

'Christ, I know you're a thespian but d'you have to dress like one of The Persuaders for fucksake?'

Maybe the black polo neck was a bad idea. He gestures to his mobile then the pub and grabs his crotch. I can guess who's on the other end.

Soon as I walk in, I know I'm right. Colin and his wife, Pam, are at the end of the bar. She's giggling into her mobile, with a naughty, nasty look on her face. Surely Colin realises? It's been years now. They used to pay Ronnie to sit down here so they could use his flat. Ian works at the bank along the road but stays in Livingston. It was a dead convenient arrangement.

Colin's over with my pint before I realise he's noticed me. He greets me with one of his crap jokes.

'How d'you get dandruff off a cunt?'

I say I don't know, he brushes my shoulder and hoots with laughter.

'Christ Col, I've not heard that one since primary.'

'You always say that.'

He tells me the arrangements, somehow managing to avoid saying Ronnie's name. It's just turned ten but the pub's packed. The jukebox is going full whack but it's still barely audible over the boom of conversation. The posties are already half cut, inventing songs of their own. Old George is shovelling coal onto the fire, which he then sits in front of, hogging the heat. Stewart the steward's at the jukebox, trying to get

June to dance. She's threatening to punch his lights out. Most of the West End Hearts are in. Just like any Saturday morning I've flown up to go to the game with Ronnie, aside from a few bad suits and the absence of Ronnie.

My first pint doesn't last five minutes. Ian's still outside. Pam's still on her mobile. Colin, still oblivious, pulls a deranged face at Frankie, who's gone self-destructive on the puggie and hasn't even noticed me. I buy a round and take him over a pint of cider. He stares through me.

'Christ man, I thought I was doing him a favour, getting him that job.'

I stick the glass in his hand to stop him shovelling more money into the machine.

'He was just chuffed to be working again, Frankie. You gave him that, Christ.'

He downs half his pint and looks very serious.

'Know what they're saying now, eh? He hadnae driven in years. I've got him fannying about the central belt in a Bedford, for fucksake. I should've checked it out, Chris. It's down to me, it really is.'

Sorry as I feel for him, I'm already looking round for Colin to rescue me. He's gone to phone his son, Paul, to see if he's coming. Paul's in the Hearts Juniors Ronnie was helping out with while he studied for his SFA licences.

The barmaid's on the phone, though, and Colin's been hijacked by singing posties. I try to sidetrack Frankie by asking about work. Frankie loves boasting about how well he's doing.

He tells me about some tenement he's doing up in Pilrig, and the great crew that's working for him, the IKEA kitchens some guy from the snooker club's sneaking out for two hundred pound a piece. Then he's back on a downer. Ronnie'd picked up some flatpacks just prior to the accident, apparently.

'I cannae handle it Chris, honestly. I know what they're all saying. I'd be saying the same.'

'Don't be daft. Christ, come on. We'll play five a side tomorrow. Beat the fucking Arabs up the Meadows. That's what Ronnie'd want.'

'But there's just four of us now.'

'So we'll get June in goals or something. Stop blaming yourself. Fuck.'

He knocks back his pint and says he'll get another while I catch up. He's obviously decided to deal with this the way he deals with everything – rat-arsed. Maggie, the manageress, only notices I'm in when she comes back with his change. She lets out a shriek, and comes running round to see me.

'Aw Christopher, how's my favourite actor?'

I don't get time to answer.

'Did you hear about Ronnie's family? The roll shop's done food. The brewery gave a few bottles for nips. But no, we're no good enough, sweetheart. Too common.'

She shakes her head and gives me her I-don't-even-want-to-go-there look. Aw, she's a Hibbie but she's brilliant.

'So what is happening afterwards? I'm not going with his lot. I'll end up in Saughton.'

'Just get as many of them back here as you can, sweetheart. The West End Hearts are coming back. This lot won't have moved. Show these snobby buggers who his real pals were.'

Thank God for that. This was Ronnie's pub. These radges were his real family. Maggie's probably glad of the extra business on a non-match day but her heart's in the right place, no pun intended. She shouts to the new barmaid to pass her fags.

'So how's the life of a Hollywood jetsetter? I watched your Taggart thing with the girls the other week. We were screaming at the telly.'

'I wasnae that bad, was I?'

She looks horrified.

'You were brilliant, sweetheart. Lauren took that photo of the pair of you to school next day to show off. Really. We watch the video when Daddy's working.'

'I only had about three lines.'

'Aye, but they were great. You really showed the boy that plays the lead up. C'mon though, what's your latest? When do I next have to set the video?'

Frankie looks pissed off and has already arsed his catch-up pint. He says he'll get us one while he's waiting. Maggie wants an answer though.

'Ocht, the usual rubbish. A Glaswegian junkie in *The Bill* – no dialogue. I just jump out a window when they knock my door down. Oh, and an alkie doctor in some

Ruth Rendell thing. I rehearsed my two lines for that on the plane.'

'The plane! Oh Christopher, what a life you lead. Aw, ma wee film star.'

Frankie shakes his head in disgust. Maggie scowls at him behind his back.

'Well before you disappear back to film land this time, I want an autograph. The girls too. They'll be worth a fortune one day.'

At least someone has a wee bit of faith in me, misguided though it is.

Colin re-appears as Frankie hands me my pint.

'I'll have one too, ta.'

'Christsake. You must smell me getting my money out, man.'

'It's the moths, Frankie,' I laugh.

'Mammoths, more like,' mutters Col.

Ian finally comes in, as Pam puts her mobile in her bag. He shouts at Frankie to get him a drink as he's handing Col his.

'Fucksake. What is it with youz and your timing?'

'Make it a double Morgan's then,' says Ian.

Frankie gets him a pint.

'You'll take what you're given, you bluenose wanker.'

Colin grins at me and points to Pam.

'What about her, Frankie? She's sitting with a glass full of ice.'

'When I see her buy a round, I'll buy her one,' says Frankie.

Pam storms off to the Ladies. Within seconds, Ian's mobile goes off and he's back outside with his drink.

'Fucking liberty,' growls Frankie. 'He's only speaking to me when he wants bevvy. See, every cunt does think it's my fault.'

Col's looking about, to see where Pam's got to. It's gone silent between Frankie and me. Luckily Ian's back in quickly.

'Sorry about that. Women, eh?' he winks. 'Anyway, good you managed to escape, Chris. Did you get shit as well? How is she? Nah, fuck women. How's acting?'

Colin starts singing the can't-get-quicker-than-a-Kwikfit-fitter song, as he always does when my job's mentioned. Bastard. He'll never let me live down my first TV appearance. It re-ignites Frankie.

'Aye, you should have heard Maggie going on about wanting his autograph. It'll be worth a fortune if he ever does anything decent, apparently.'

Col's still singing the stupid jingle in my other ear. Ian, Rangers bastard that he is, at least defends me.

'You can laugh. I sent Lorraine through to Glasgow the other week. Paul Gascoigne was doing a book-signing. You should've seen the price George Best's book was going for on eBay the day of his funeral. She got me five, so I know who *will* be laughing when *he* pops his clogs.'

Frankie's reached the bottom of another glass.

'Get Ewan McGregor here to sign some beer mats, then murder him. We'll all be minted.'

'Aye, well you've got the track record. We'll leave that up to you, eh, Frankie?'

I half expect him to clock Ian one, but incredibly, he keeps on at me.

'Fuck you. And him – too busy playing smackie, wife-beating twat-heids to send Ronnie that ticket for his last Hearts game.'

I let it go. He's right. The realisation that Ronnie must have told them all about it makes me feel like utter shite.

Ian tries to shut him up by getting another round. Frankie's been going on so much he still has a full pint, but accepts one anyway. Pam's up at the jukebox, so Colin's trying to charm the new barmaid with his crap jokes. Who can blame him, considering?

'See when we get back, Julie, will you comfort me against your bosom?'

'Aye sure. I'll suffocate you,' she says, pulling pints without even looking up.

Billy, the grouchiest man on the planet, comes over to ask if we're going to the funeral. Like, we were only his best friends!

'Nah, we're auditioning for the St Bride's production of *Reservoir Dogs*.'

The dour bastard blanks me and says he's going with Duncan the drunken taxi driver. I have a fleeting fantasy about them crashing, then feel bad for thinking such a thing in the circumstances.

Ian points at his watch. The hearse is due outside the stadium in ten minutes. We all have drink left, but he buys us each a double, regardless. Frankie looks stunned. We make a toast to Ronnie then knock them back in one. It's shocking, really, driving pissed to the funeral of a best pal killed in a car crash. Ian's a careful driver, though. Even when he's off his face. And it's not like I can drive so I can hardly criticise.

It's after five-to when we leave. Lots of folk are already away. Even a few of the posties have gone with Stewart the steward and June. As we stumble out the back door, I suddenly think, wait, Ronnie must still be in the bogs. Then I remember.

The hearse and limo drive by as we come out of the pub. I see Ronnie's horrible sister staring out disapprovingly as it passes. Frankie's staggering about the place as well. Typical.

We pile into Ian's car but Frankie insists first on having a piss behind a van. Fucksake. We'll miss the minute's silence outside Tynecastle. He's twenty feet away, the engine's running but I can still hear it, gushing out the twat. He finally wobbles towards us, banging his head on the way in. Ian's seething.

'Christ Frankie, I know you're a Celtic supporter, but do you have to act like a fucking weedgie all the time?'

It's not until we turn into the street I realise there's about two dozen folk standing outside the front of the pub. A sea of black, white and maroon. Mourners with scarfs; regulars; some of the West End crowd; the boys from the bookies; some parents from the juniors; the old morning crew; even a couple of radges from Stratties and the sports shop.

'This is my story,
this is my song,
Follow the Hearts and you can't go wrong . . .'

I get an instant lump in my throat.

'. . . Oh some say that Celtic and Rangers are grand
But the boys in maroon are the best in the land . . .'

'The fucking hairs are up on the back of my neck. And I hate the Jambo cunts,' says Ian.

Frankie's shaking his head, shiny-eyed.

'I'll waste that Range-Rover, Barbour-jacketed bastard. See when it comes to court. I'll take a fucking knife.'

'. . . H-E-A . . . R-T-S,
If you cannae spell it then here's what it says . . .'

Colin, the Hibbie, is just gawping at them.

'Christ, Ronnie'd fucking love this.'

By the time we get along to the stadium, the hearse, limo and a couple of other cars are already parked. No sooner have we stopped behind them, though, they take off. It's only just turned eleven. It's like they've seen us and changed their minds.

'Fuck it Ian, have our own minute's silence. There's plenty time, yet.'

He kills the engine and we synchronise watches. It's thirty seconds past eleven. I look across at Tynecastle, half expecting Ronnie to knock on the window and ask us what the fuck we're doing. I'm getting choked up again, so I try to think of any old shite to get Ronnie and his brilliant laugh out of my head but it's like trying to give up smoking. There suddenly doesn't seem to be anything else to think about.

When Frankie's mobile goes off, with about fifteen seconds to go, I'm sort of relieved. Fields of fucking Athenry though. What a twat. He fumbles to switch it off.

As soon as the minute's up, Ian leans over and grabs him by the ear.

'Just make sure it's off during the service, or I'll break your fucking neck.'

For once, Frankie seems genuinely embarrassed.

'Like I'm that ignorant, Ian, eh? Gimme a break.'

As we drive towards Mortonhall, it goes quiet in the car. Like we're afraid to speak in case it sparks off another argument. It reminds me of the weird, stunned silence on the bus back from the '98 Cup Final. I was there with Ronnie. After thirty-five years supporting Hearts, when victory finally arrived, it was like we didn't know the words. It struck us temporarily dumb. I stare out the window at a passing Edinburgh that'll never quite be the same again. The streets seem strangely hushed. Even the roads are quiet. Unsurprisingly, it's Frankie that breaks the silence.

'Put some fucking sounds on, eh? This no speaking's doing my head in.'

For once he goes unchallenged. I think we're all starting to feel the same. The radio gets switched on just in time to hear Meat Loaf screech the immortal line,

'. . . now I'm dying at the bottom of a pit in the blazing sun . . .'

'Brilliant,' mutters Ian, quickly changing stations. *'Everybody Hurts'* is next up. We groan in unison. I usually love that song but not today. And certainly not *'Stan'*, which is Forth FM's offering. Ian gives up and sticks on one of the dance music stations. We all hate dance music, but at least it doesn't make me think anything other than what the fuck is that?

By the time we get to the crematorium, the coffin and congregation are already inside. The undertakers are about to close the doors and come out for a fag. Ian double parks and we speed-walk down the path, past a row of floral tributes.

'Christ, did anyone get a wreath?'

Ian shrugs. 'Like he cares now.'

Colin agrees. 'Aye, fuck that. We'll do what we arranged. That'll be fine.'

'Aye, whap those fucking Arabs tomorrow,' grunts Frankie, 'Here, hang on, I need another piss.'

Ian yanks him by the arm.

'Just fucking move it. It'll only last ten minutes. They've got the next one to fry at quarter to twelve.'

The doors are closed behind us. It's in the smallest crematorium, so there's already half the Hearts bus standing at the back. I don't want to see the curtains at the side of the coffin tremble as it goes down anyway. It always makes me want to laugh, for some horrible reason. I can't see his family from here either, which suits me fine.

The female minister gives a wee spiel about Ronnie that she probably does a dozen times a day. As none of us were asked, it's all about family, work, morality and perseverance. She makes him sound like a fucking Mormon.

She makes us pray and then mime along to a hymn that no-one seems to know. There aren't any hymn books at the back, which makes it even more ridiculous. What's all this crap got to do with Ronnie anyway? They should play some Rod Stewart or Stevie Wonder. We should be singing a Hearts song. Something he liked, surely? Ronnie didn't even believe in God. Who does these days apart from Ann Widdecombe and Bono?

We're forced into a final prayer, before the organ starts up, the doors are opened and it's over. You're supposed to wait for the family to leave first, but we can't get out of there quick enough. There's too many at the back for all that ceremonious shit. No danger of that anyway as Frankie's straight behind a tree.

'I don't believe that bastard,' mutters Col.

A group of kids spot him, and start laughing and pointing. Luckily Ian misses this as he's back on his mobile. Jesus, does he never give his dick a day-off? Ronnie's family are too busy giving funny handshakes at the chapel door to even notice we're here. I stand well back to keep it that way.

Colin's laddie, Paul's here with the rest of the Hearts juniors. He's a Hibbie, like Col, but at least he plays for the right team. Col's trying to get him to come with us but he's got a training session this afternoon.

'It's the first one without Ronnie, Dad. I sort of want to be there.'

Col squeezes his shoulder.

'Aye, you're right. Good laddie.'

I feel a stab of pride for the boy and a sadness that Ronnie never had any kids. Then Frankie's back over doing up his zip.

'So what's it like playing for the enemy, Paul? Never tempted to do a bit of a Bruce Grobbelaar?'

I have to hold Colin back.

'What do your kids do like, Frankie? You don't even fucking know, do you, so shut the fuck up.'

Now Frankie's going for Colin. Ian swats him away with his mobile.

'Christ, have a bit of respect, the pair of you, eh? They already think we're scumbags. Dinnae confirm it, fucksake.'

Too late. Over his shoulder I see Ronnie's cunt of a sister

heading our way. She's dabbing away tears, but has an expression of false sincerity that would make Peter Mandelson blush.

'She must have an onion in her bag,' I mumble as she walks up to Ian.

'I just wanted to thank you all for coming. We didn't expect many people, so we appreciate you making the effort.'

What's she on about? It was like an Edinburgh derby in that crematorium. Patronising bitch.

'Best turnout I've ever seen,' says Colin. 'Ronnie had lots of good friends. My laddie's in the juniors he worked with. They're all here as well.'

Without acknowledging him, she says there's a buffet for twenty booked at the Orwell, so there's only room for family and close friends.

'As I said, though, thank you all for coming anyway.'

I see Frankie snarling. Ian pushes in front of him.

'That's fine. There's a big function at the pub for everybody.'

'How appropriate. I suppose they'll need all the business they can get, now Ronnie's gone.'

The tears are gone. And so, thank fuck, is she. Again, I seek solace in brief, inappropriate car crash fantasies.

'Surely Ronnie must've been swapped at birth,' Colin speculates.

Frankie agrees. 'We should've just stayed in the pub. That was a fucking farce. Hear her going on about Ronnie like he was some kind of alkie. Ugly auld trout.'

It seems like a good time to leave. We tell a few folk we'll see them back at the pub, then get in the car.

'D'you think that bitch'll get the flat? Fuck, just the thought of her nosing through the place and chucking half his things out. That can't be right, surely?'

I know Ian still has keys for Ronnie's place. I wonder if he means we should salvage some personal stuff before she gets her claws in. On second thoughts, he's probably more worried that his love nest is about to go down the plughole. I wouldn't be surprised if Pam and him were at it up there before Ronnie was even cold.

'Thank fuck that Tanya left him before he had time to marry her. She'd probably have turned it into a knocking shop,' says Col.

God, I'd forgotten about Tanya. Another of Ian's conquests. I notice his shoulders stiffening up when she's mentioned. Thank fuck Ronnie never found out.

We drive back through the wooded path from the crematorium then turn right, out of town. Frankie's confused.

'What are you playing at? Fuck the scenic route, I'm gasping on a pint.'

I assumed he'd been told about the arrangement.

'Just shut it, eh? It won't take long,' says Ian, turning onto the bypass.

We pass a sign for Hillend. Frankie seems to click and slumps back down in his seat. We're there in a couple of minutes.

It seems to appear out of nowhere, even though I'm expecting it. The right side of Lothianburn junction is scattered with flowers, rosettes and scarfs. I feel sick and sad and proud, all at once. As Ian parks on a grass verge behind the junction, a horrible sense that we shouldn't be here starts to grip me. But the rest of them get out, so I have to follow. I don't want to have to try and explain.

We cross over to what's left of the fence. I feel weak and shell-shocked, as if *I've* just stepped out of a car crash. Even the police cordon has cards, match tickets, Hearts keyrings hung on it. The grass is black, oily and charred and there's pieces of twisted metal and broken glass everywhere. Every time a car goes past on the bypass, it makes me shudder. This is horrible. I want away from here.

When Ian produces a half bottle of Grouse and paper cups from a carrier bag, my instinct is to start running.

'We'll have this and then go,' he whispers, handing us each an equal dram.

I take mine over to what's left of the fence. I just want to be on my own until this is over. Lighting a fag is a bad move though. They're all over, wanting one. Ian and Colin don't even smoke.

Thankfully, Ian takes his and goes to sit in the car.

Frankie goes wandering off down the road to deal with his own demons.

Colin crosses over to the other side of the junction and sits with his back to us, facing the black hulk of the Pentlands.

I slug back some whisky, close my eyes and try to block the present out. Try to let my mind take me to some happier time, with Ronnie. The Ronnie I want to remember, on the bus home from the '98 Cup Final.

It was strangely subdued to begin with. Like we couldn't take in the fact that we'd actually won. It wasn't till we reached the outskirts of Edinburgh that realisation started to sink in and excitement break out, like a rash. The singing started up. First just a few of us, unfamiliar with our new song,

'We won the cup, we won the cup . . .'

By Sighthill, they started coming out onto the streets. An old woman with a zimmer, maroon-clad kids on their fathers' shoulders, old boys waving flags out of windows, gangs of bairns, draped in banners.

'We won the cup, we won the cup . . .'

Pubs and shops emptying onto the road to welcome us back to Gorgie. The great, big noise of hooters, cheering, chanting, car horns, drums. The bus shuddering as we stomped our way home, singing and sobbing and hoping the fuck it wasn't just a dream.

'WE WON THE CUP, WE WON THE CUP . . .'

Ian starts blaring the horn.

'C'mon, we better be making a move.'

I wait till the tears stop, then stand up, raise my cup to the sky and get back into the car.

Victims

HE WAS DRIVING home from his late shift in the early hours of a Sunday morning when he first saw her. She was staggering around the West End, trying to thumb down a free lift, gesturing angrily at any taxi that unwittingly slowed down. Two miles down the road, unable to shift the vision of her from his mind, he'd reversed.

She wasn't hard to find – only a few yards from where he'd originally passed her, hurling insults at a carload of whistling Arabs. He felt extremely chivalrous as she climbed into his car, told him she'd run out of money and asked if he'd take her to her parents' house in Colinton.

When they arrived there, she told him to park in the lane next to the rugby fields, as she didn't feel like going home yet. They sat talking until it started to get light, listening to the same Stones cassette over and over again until at 5.30 he told her he'd have to go pick up his children from the neighbours.

Silently, she got out of the car and gestured him to follow. His brief pang of confusion was surpassed by a compulsion to do exactly as she asked. He beeped the doors locked and walked quickly after her. When she sensed him immediately behind her she stepped off the pavement and squeezed through a hole in the fence to the fields. He followed automatically. At the side of the pitch, she lay down on the grass and spread her legs in invitation. As he bent down to join her though, she pushed him away.

'No, you stand there and do it to yourself.'

Momentary reservations were dismissed at the sight of her hand circling inside her knickers. Dropping his trousers, he did as she asked, as she lay watching and chuckling. Afterwards, she let him lie next to her, finishing herself off as she stared at his semen on the wildlife.

He was smitten.

Despite giving him her phone number, she had no intention of seeing him again. Her mother was used to scummy-sounding men phoning up for her over the weekends, and always told them they had the wrong number without her ever having to ask.

But the telephone began ringing at 10.30 as she sat having a piss; watching a whirling blue ball diffuse seaweed essence into her steaming bath. Her mother was still zonked out on her tablets and dead to the world. She worried it might be someone decent.

He stammered something about wanting to see her. He'd been stammering the night before but she'd put it down to nerves. She found the idea that he did it all the time distasteful. She couldn't even recall what he looked like but the probability of his ugliness and subsequent desperation gave her a thrill. He pleaded with her to see him. She countered with a line of insultingly unlikely excuses, enjoying the hopeless tone in his voice, until he suddenly spluttered out that two years previously, his wife had been killed in a road accident in which he was driving the car and that he had been unable to g-g-get hard s-s-since then until n-now. She stifled a yawn but he carried on pleading and drilling words endlessly until she decided he might be fun to torment a bit more and submitted.

He was to pick her up on the other side of the road from her parents' house at 6.00 that evening, but when she walked past the window at 5.15 he was already there. From a distance, his ugliness was disappointingly conventional and she could hear the Stones tape from the night before blaring out the car window. But, having fallen out further with the friend she'd walked out on prior to meeting him, she needed someone to take it out on. He'd told her he was loaded. She knew with people like him that meant a shitty twenty grand that didn't even cover the mortgage, but if he wanted to get into more debt with her for a week or so, so be it. She checked her reflection as she sniffed at a bottle of poppers. Who could blame him, she thought, grinding her perfectly capped teeth. Why not give the poor gimp a treat?

She kept him waiting until 7.25.

He seemed unconcerned as he managed to stop ogling her long enough to drive them to a small hotel in the New Town where he filled her with double gin and tonics. Although frequently but unintentionally amusing company, his stammer still repulsed her. He told her, with pantomime candour, that he worked for a s-s-s-s-security f-f-f-firm, made a fortune in b-b-back-back-handers but that the less-ess-ess she knew about it the b-b-better. Nonetheless, his awfulness tickled her as she connived ways she could help rid him of such a clandestine financial burden.

In the hotel bar, he spoke louder than necessary so that other people would look over and see them together. He gawped, transfixed, as she told him she'd dreamt about him. About him! She'd been driving him very fast along a country road as he fingered her. For the first time she appeared sad, as she told him that she couldn't drive so that could never come true. How much she wanted to learn to drive but didn't have the confidence. Made foolish by six pints of Murphy's, he suggested they drink up and he give her a lesson.

An hour later, as she stalled and started the car round one of the Gyle's vast, deceptively beautiful monstrosities, he supped on her breasts as she brutalised his Citroen's inner mechanisms. With her tits as a spur, he blankly allowed her to circle the building a few dozen times before late night security had to finally pause their late night poker game and pretend to be bothered.

She drove off, at his direction, into the wasteland of Broomhouse – her body pumping with the adrenaline of getting off the treadmill into the mire. She parked outside some bucket of a flat, breathless from it all. Absolutely alive. Launching her lips onto his, she forced his hand inside her bra, clamping it round her breast. Brushing his lips against her neck, he whispered that he l-l-loved her. He loved her so m-much. It h-h-hurt him because he loved her so m-much. Despite the alarm bells ringing in her ears, she unzipped his trousers, took out his small flabby penis and sucked him off with the painfully slow professionalism of experience.

When she looked up again there were tears rolling down his pasty cheeks and she realised that his gasps had been sobs. She felt a bizarre pang of affection sautéed gently in disgust.

'Nobody's ever done that to me before,' he said, without stammering.

She bit her lip and tried not to laugh, till his eyes suddenly collapsed somewhere and he blurted out that his wife was in fact alive and cooking but he, poor sap, was in love with HER now . . .
and had
never felt
anything
like

this
can't
stop
thinking
about
please
please
please
feel
the
same
say
you
feel
the
same
please
please
please
love . . .

She waited for him to shut up and start stammering again. God, how she wanted him to stammer, but he just kept on this awful, monotonous, dreadful, incessant shitty noise. She belched his spunk back in his face without a let-up. She reminded him that he'd only known her fifteen hours, but he just continued simpering and insisting that he loved her and he'd never felt like this before; that marriage wasn't a word but a sentence. She remembered seeing that cliché printed on an enormous badge at the counter of the card shop she'd been in the other day. He was immediately an idiot. Not the sort of idiot she liked to humiliate for fun any more. Just some worthless cunt she immediately felt sick about being alone with.

But he was on a stuttering, fuckering roll now that wouldn't stop. His family meant nothing to him any more. He yanked his wallet out of the glove compartment and thrust two gnarled photos at her. One was of a blonde, bland woman in her thirties – the other of two fat, ghastly kids, grinning affectedly in their school uniforms. Melodramatically retrieving the photo of the woman from her, he flicked a cheap, orange disposable lighter with an unfeasibly large flame and set light to the edge of it. Fumes and black smoke quickly engulfed the blonde and he threw her out the window. The foul smell caught the back of her throat, partly from the photo and partly from a now singed patch on the ceiling of the car. Despite herself though, she felt impressed and gestured at the photo of the kids on his lap.

'What about them? Don't you love me more than them?'

Despite his look of broken disbelief, he picked up the photo and set the lighter to it as well. Grinning as they burned, she felt almost more attracted to him for having lied so mercilessly in the first place.

The following day she let him pick her up from work at midday and drive her to his house while his wife was away for a pampering session at the local spa (his treat) and the brood were at school. Wandering through the house she grimaced at family photos and rummaged through drawers looking for bank statements while he tried to interest her in some lunch.

Upstairs, sitting on his marital bed, she stirred her finger round the water in the goldfish bowl on the bedside table.

'Jesus Christ, has this thing ever been cleaned out?'

'It's h-h-hers,' he struggled, trying to make out the frantic fish amidst the camouflage of filth, 'I forgot it was th-th-there.'

Swiping the muck off her finger onto the carpet, she stood up and walked out of the room, sniggering.

Following her into his daughter's bedroom, he watched as she threw herself onto the rainbow coloured quilt, kicked her shoe off and ground her foot into his groin.

'Do you really love me more than them?'

He gasped in affirmation.

'Would you leave them for me? Never see them again?'

He moved onto the bed beside her.

'Is that what you want? If that's what you want . . .'

She laughed at his bug-eyed ignorance, lay back on the bed and opened her legs. Unfastening himself, he tried to climb on top of her but like before, she pushed him away and told him she just wanted to watch. Frustrated, he knelt on the bed between her legs and pulled at his cock as she frigged herself.

'Is that where you want to go?' she smirked.

'Let me, please,' he gasped, trying again to get on top and penetrate her. She pushed him away again, but this time he didn't give in. Quickly grabbing her wrists behind her head, he forced all his weight upon her so she couldn't move.

'Get off me you fucking creep,' she screamed, jerking one hand free and smacking him round the face with it, tearing at his hair. He kept going, trying to get inside her but only managing to rub his cock roughly against the entrance to her cunt. It was painful but he couldn't stop now. He crunched his lips against hers and felt her spitting onto his mouth. He sucked it in and swallowed. As she struggled to free her mouth from his, she managed to bite down hard on his eyebrow. By the time he pulled away in pain, he was already ejaculating onto her. She squealed and wiped at the mess, rubbing it onto his face, pounding her fists on the side of his head. He stood up, stammering apologies as he struggled back into his trousers.

'Why couldn't you j-j-just let me? I l-l-l-love you.'

All she could think was that she desperately wanted to come. She'd wanted it to continue. Her delight at having turned him bad so quickly had enlivened her, but instead she feigned offence and pretended to be hurt and horrified.

'I thought you were a good person. How could you do that?'

'Y-y-y-y-y-y-yuh-yuh . . .'

'Oh just shut the fuck up, eh?'

Getting up from the bed, she noticed a line of spunk glinting across the duvet cover. She smiled as he followed her back downstairs, imagining how the stammering shit was going to explain that when his missus got back from her pampering session.

Disappointingly though, when they next met, the stain wasn't mentioned. Instead he was full of ideas about them moving in together. They had holiday money saved he could use for a deposit on a flat. In a matter of just five days he'd realised his marriage was over. There was no point pretending any more.

Much as she knew such declarations were the words of a sad, deluded idiot, the offer was slightly tempting. For years, when she went through housing schemes and poor areas on the bus or train, she'd fantasised about getting fucked by some rough-necked nobody in one of these filthy, low-ceilinged, high-rise coffins. She was desperate to move from her parents' house but could never hold onto enough money to save up the deposit and first month's rent for a place of her own. Her mother, though only semi-conscious for most of the time, interfered in her life too much – searching her room, opening her mail then going berserk at the things she subsequently discovered.

It would be worth it just to see the look of horror on her mother's face when she told her she was moving in with some jumped-up fucking porter. She just needed to humour him till he signed the lease. Then he could do whatever the fuck he wanted. Besides, he worked shifts. They wouldn't even need to see each other.

Although the idea was growing on her, she remained aloof as this seemed to make him all the more persistent; however, this soon bored her. As he drove her home from work the following evening, she told him to arrange it all and let her know when they could move in. Luckily the lights were at red. In floods of tears, he pulled the ring from his index finger and pressed it earnestly into the palm of her hand.

'Please, I want you to have this. It was my dad's.'

She placed the large, ugly band of silver on her right thumb. It was little more than a ring-pull but she forced a smile and wondered if he was any good at decorating. He was still in tears, muttering and stuttering about love, when he dropped her off at her house. It was Parents' Evening at his kids' school and he had to look after them while his wife attended it. Although reluctant to leave her, he said he wanted to spend some time with Ross and Mandy before he abandoned them. It offended her to hear their names. It was way too much information. There'd be no more sentimental shit like that once they got their flat.

It was her birthday the following day. He arranged to pick her up after work to take her for a double celebratory meal. She'd already arranged a party with friends but planned to meet him prior to this and get drunk at his expense, although as far away from where she was meeting her friends as possible. If anyone ever saw her with him, she'd just die. She blocked the unpleasant thought from her mind.

When she glanced out of her office window at 4.30 the next day, however, he wasn't there. Although he wasn't due until 5.00 she sensed something was wrong. He usually liked to creep around outside for hours before they were due to meet. He said it made him feel close to her.

She stayed in the office until 5.45, watching with growing fury as a large, grey cloud drifted slowly in her direction, opening up just as it reached her street. Livid as she ran towards the bus stop in driving rain, she swore she would never see him again.

Arriving home to her mother in a rage about unpaid Visa bills or some such shit, she locked herself in the shower and beat her fists off the tiles. What a bastard. She felt like crying, but she never cried. She refused to cry over a worthless twat like him. It was just the uncertainty over what she was supposed to be doing now. It was nothing to do with feelings. No way had he got to her. It was her fucking birthday. Fucking bastard.

In her bedroom, she tore into a pile of unopened presents, looking for the little black dress her stepfather had bought her. Throwing everything else across the room without even looking at it, she found his parcel and squeezed into the dress. Her mother came through as she was admiring her reflection in the mirror, seeking reconciliation and full of compliments about the new outfit. She gestured to the discarded presents.

'Ocht, I'm in a hurry. I'll look later.'

Despite being far too early to meet her friends, she got a taxi into the West End. Checking the time on the clock above Frazers, she entered the busy pub. There was an hour and a half to kill, but what the hell, it was her birthday. As she tried to get the barman's attention, she caught the eye of a man standing joking with friends. Still staring, she walked over and asked him the time.

'Time you stopped waiting on whoever you're waiting on and had a drink with me,' he said hopefully. His friends all laughed. She walked back to where she'd been standing and ordered a drink. This was a joke. Where was that fucking bastard? She just wanted to know.

Checking she had change, she called the number she'd noted down off a phone bill she'd found in his house. Almost immediately, a tearful woman answered and nervously asked who was calling, so she hung up.

She hadn't liked him anyway. He was just some wanker who bought her drink, let her drive his car and treat him like shit. The idea that she'd almost moved in with the moron made her glad he was gone. She hoped he was dead. Glancing back across at the man she'd asked the time, she noticed him still smiling over at her. She smiled back. Edinburgh was full of unbalanced arseholes, waiting to be pushed.

The Boxroom

AS THE COACH lurched towards the castle, Carol looked at her mother and Uncle Len with disgust. Uncle Len was not a real uncle. Carol's mother occasionally took lodgers in the spare room, except the spare room was meant to be Carol's room. Carol, therefore, had to sleep in the boxroom. If she was not bitter enough about having to sleep in this windowless cupboard, she was frequently disturbed by snoring from next door. Uncle Len had first stayed there with his wife for a week one summer but she had since died. Uncle Len mentioned a broken heart and now visited every few months, free of charge. He was adopted. An orphaned husband uncle. His snoring was so loud that the glass in his door rattled.

Sometimes, while Uncle Len and her mother were having one of their private talks in her parents' bedroom, Carol would tiptoe into the spare room and take money from Uncle Len's purse. Although she did this almost daily, she would always begin trembling uncontrollably as she undid the purse's metal clasp. Her ears used to pop, as if she had been blowing up too many balloons and she could not hear properly. After taking the money she would go back to the boxroom and lie down, until her legs stopped feeling strange. Then she would pull the stitching out of her teddy bear, insert the coins and stitch him up again.

She had only recently been moved back to the boxroom. When she was very young, she had suffered from asthma. When she was first moved from her parents' room into the boxroom at the age of five she would remain awake until she heard her father leaving for his work at the brewery at 4.30 each morning. Then she'd run through to spend the last few hours of darkness in her mother's bed. This was of course unsatisfactory. She began acting out asthma attacks as she was put to bed each night. Her parents fretted terribly over their sickly little creation. For a couple of nights Carol's father slept in the boxroom and let Carol sleep with her mother. Every time Carol was returned to the boxroom the asthma would return. Her father gave up his bed for a week, then a month, then years. Carol was thus an only child.

One night Carol said goodnight to her parents and went up to her mother's bed. She could not sleep as she had a terrible itch. She scratched until she was raw but the itch persisted. Eventually it was too painful to continue scratching. She began rubbing rather than scratching. The rubbing relieved the itch but when she stopped, the itch returned. She rubbed persistently for several minutes until something peculiar happened. Carol, for no reason, suddenly imagined a policeman doing his toilet in a pram. Her ears popped and she began trembling, but this time it was nice. She had felt similar feelings before if she lay down and needed the toilet for as long as she could. Carol forgot about the itch.

The next night, Carol's mother was tired and came up to bed early. Once her mother switched the light out, Carol began the rubbing again. She rubbed for several minutes wondering if it would ever happen again. It did. The following evening Carol was moved back to the boxroom.

Adults are strange. Why do they assume children enjoy day trips? How could they believe Carol would be remotely interested in spending the day walking around a mouldy old castle? She had enough of that sort of rubbish at school. She would much prefer to lie in the boxroom needing the toilet, or sit in the back garden watching her old neighbour walk about his house, or go up to the wasteland at the top of her street and climb trees.

The coach rounded the loch on its way towards the castle. Carol noticed an oldish man four rows down from her. Immediately she could not take her eyes off him. He was tall and thin with greying hair, wearing a brown suit and smoking a pipe. Distinguished. He was talking to a very old, small woman who looked as if she might die at any minute.

The two figures were separated from everyone else by a cloud of smoke from the man's pipe. Carol assumed the old woman must be his mother. If so then he must not be married. Why would a man take his mother on a coach trip if he had a wife? He made Carol feel itchy. She was eleven years old but was tall for her age and could pass for fourteen when she wore her good coat.

On arrival at the castle, Uncle Len hobbled with delight when Carol suddenly seemed intrigued and asked if she could go and explore by herself. They pointed out the tea garden and arranged to meet her there later.

The next two hours were spent with the man constantly in her sights. The old lady's slow progress meant that Carol had time to stare at his reflection in the glass of numerous cases holding jewels and suits of armour. If he seemed to linger longer than normal at a particular place, Carol would study it afterwards. She tried to build up some sort of picture of what kind of man he was. One such exhibit was a painting of *Faust Descending into Hell.* Where did the Devil live, she wondered? Probably somewhere in London.

Carol was relieved when the man and the old lady eventually began making their way down the stairs towards the tea garden. The castle was dark and clammy and she was beginning to feel uncomfortable. She watched through the hedge as the old lady was helped into a seat on the lawn by the man. He went across to the tea garden. Carol sat at a nearby table between the old lady and the hedge. She toyed with her hair and leaned back in the chair, trying to look sophisticated. The man returned with a tray, moving across the grass in slow motion. He smiled as he approached. Was it directed at Carol? She was sure it was. In case he should look over again she assumed a constant grin. It was a look she had practised often in the bathroom mirror. He poured two cups of tea from the pot then raised a cup to his lips, his pinkie erect. He really was very refined.

Although she needed the toilet she decided to wait until her mother and Uncle Len reappeared. She could not risk losing such an excellent view of this elegant creature. Staring intently at him, still smiling, she pressed her thighs close together. She felt her bladder twitching in a very pleasant way. She felt sorry that the man could not also experience such sensations.

By the time her mother appeared she was beginning to perspire. Uncle Len limped across to buy the afternoon tea. He suffered from some old person's disease and was also in need of a hip replacement operation. Carol could not understand why people like him were not just shot. Her mother gestured for her to go and help her uncle with the tray.

'Hang on, there's a queue. I'll go over when he's paid for it!' She savoured her last few moments alone with the man until her mother nudged her roughly out of her thoughts and pointed to Uncle Len, who was now tottering across with the tray. Carol felt embarrassed to be seen with such a person.

Her mother again shouted at Carol to help him. Her tone was so harsh that the man and his mother looked around. Carol stood up, thoroughly humiliated, and then a sudden wave of strangeness flushed over her. She squeezed her toilet muscles but it didn't work. She simpered and began running in the direction of the toilets. Urine was dripping from the vast dark patch growing on her lime green trousers. As she bolted, she saw the man nudge his mother and they looked over. Carol ran, sobbing.

When her mother knocked on the door of the public toilet several minutes later, Carol was standing, naked from the waist down, wringing her knickers and trousers in the sink, still sobbing.

'I can't go home . . . I can't go home . . . they all saw me . . . I can't go back on the coach . . . they all saw me . . . I'll have to stay here . . . you go home . . . leave me here!'

Carol refused to leave the toilets until the coach was due to depart. Uncle Len asked the driver to wait as his niece was ill. Eventually she boarded the coach with her mother's arm around her shoulders and a travelling rug around her waist. There was quiet as she made her way to her seat. Uncle Len was sitting directly opposite the man with the pipe. The old lady was tugging at his jacket to find out what was wrong. The man looked inquiringly at

Carol then at Uncle Len. Uncle Len leaned towards him, and as the coach stammered into motion Carol heard him whisper: 'I think she's on the rag.'

Destination Anywhere

I'M HATING THIS but the money is good and the ghouls carrying trays of champagne are very generous. I've already taken enough photos – the ones the magazine wants – just that right mixture of urban cool and in-crowd exclusionism. I would prefer to take their pictures now when they're coked-up, gaggled and clucking at each other as they fall about the place, but I was told to put the camera away after the initial unveiling of the shitty paintings as, according to the artist, it inhibits networking.

I'm only here because Rick, my friend from college who usually does the paper's society page, is in Somalia photographing a celebrity chef for an African cooking special commissioned by Sainsbury's. My work generally involves images of urban squalor – bleak monochrome images of hospitals, terminal illness and death; NHS profiles so to speak. I'm working towards a major exhibition of my work. Not a few pictures in a café or coffee shop but in a place like this except with real people, rather than this bunch of screaming squirrels. I aim to be the great lensman laureate of the British underclasses; the British Nick Ut; to one day win the Pulitzer Prize; to find my own Kim Phuc. I even use the same camera – a Nikon, Kodak film and 35mm lens – that Ut used. The photo I'm currently proudest of is of three Armenians – man, woman and emaciated hopeless-looking child – crammed into a sleeping bag together and waiting to be smuggled back to France. I was only in Dover for an away day across the Channel for cheap fags. A photographer needs to be lucky like that.

I know I should leave soon but the champagne is being pushed and I'm starting to enjoy getting speedily pissed and laughing to myself about how fucking awful the paintings are. The drink is going through me though. I've been to the toilet three times in an hour. Each time, the artist has been in there, lining up powder. At first I was torn between taking his photo or smacking his head against the wall. Then on my third visit to the bogs, I accepted the offer of a line.

I look at myself in the mirror and like what I see. I want to keep looking but the pale, sweaty artist comes into focus again, breaking my lovely moment of self love. Bastard. I've not felt so confident in ages. I almost feel good enough to speak to Sophie. I should leave now and go home and finally tell her it like it is.

As I walk back through to the gaggle, they seem even

more pathetic. It boosts my feeling of confidence even more. Just a little more Dutch courage and I'll go. Grabbing two glasses of champagne off a tray, I push through, looking for a focus. I am ready to erupt with brilliant insights. Despite the fact I'm starving, I have to reject the offered canapés as I have a glass in each hand. Am I actually starving anyway? I'm not even hungry, really. Sophie was going to cook us dinner. Chucking down some more champagne, it makes me nauseous.

I should go. After this, I'll go. Emptying the first of the glasses, I stare at a dreadful painting that looks like a used tampon in a bag of sugar. It is called 'Untitled 5'. I feel deeply offended in some way and feel myself bubbling with loathing.

Someone takes me by the arm. Do I know her? She's the first person I've looked at and not hated for the past hour. Where do I know her from? I can't remember. She squeezes me.

'So, d'you like this one? You've been staring at it for ages . . .'

I stare at her blankly.

'. . . I think it's bullshit. Don't you think? They're all bullshit?'

I realise I don't know her. Tonight is the only place I know her from. She came in with the newspaper editor and his hangers on. I overheard two of them earlier, fighting over which of them the newspaper editor would choose tonight. The girl looks like the daughter of one of his set. I squint at the awful painting again.

'On the other hand, anyone rich and pretentious enough to shell out for crap like that deserves to get ripped off – ten grand, Christ.'

I'm pleased with this comment. This is not art. Not my art. Emperor's new clothes guff like this. The girl's still smiling anyway.

'So why d'you take photos of them? I saw you earlier.'

I drain the second glass.

'I'm just doing a mate a favour. Nothing to do with me. You've got to be joking. Think I'm interested in dross like that?'

She shrugs.

'You're still here. They can't be that bad.'

I grab two more glasses off a passing tray and hand her one. She doesn't look eighteen but everyone's so up their own arses I can't imagine they care.

'Believe me, even the artist can't stand them.'

'What, Christian? Christian's ok. I don't like his pictures but he's cute.'

I gulp back more drink.

'If having a rolled up tenner glued to your nose, slumped in the bogs is cute these days, then yeah, he is cuteness personified.'

She looks confused. I finish my drink.

'Forget it. I'm off. You were right. What the hell am I still doing here?'

I'm feeling a bit giddy. I have to go. I can't keep avoiding things like this. I just have to go home, and tell Sophie, and deal with however she reacts. Don't drink any more. I'm not used to anything this place has to offer. Documenting despair doesn't pay for much champagne and coke. As I try to leave though, the girl tightens her grip on my arm.

'Hey wait. I'm enjoying talking to you. I want to hear about what you do.'

I look at her properly for the first time, for about two seconds, imagining her naked. Nah. She's thick-set and just a kid. Some men would no doubt go there but not me. Since Sophie took me in as a flatmate a year ago I've been unable to even consider any other woman. Since my first night there when we talked for hours. That's the problem. She's become too much of a friend. It's making me ill. Go now, Glen, when you've got a bit of extra nerve about you. Why am I such a cowardly twat around her?

As the girl's just grabbed another two glasses from somewhere though, I figure the more courage the better. In fact, if she's going to hold me captive, I'm going back to the gents to see if sadlad is still feeling generous.

I stumble back through the crowd again. There's someone in the cubicle but otherwise the toilets are empty. I'm pissed off I didn't come back sooner, but there's still traces of powder where the artist had been sitting. I wipe it all over with my fingers then rub it round my gums. It tastes of disinfectant.

As I leave the toilets, I notice the artist talking to

some queeny old hack I know from the *Evening News*. For months now, I've been convinced the hack is about to succumb to AIDS, though everyone else that knows him denies it. He stares at me, trying to remember who I am, then winks a gay wink. I pray my analysis of his health is correct.

I make for the door. The girl is still standing beside it, looking through the crowd for me. Her face brightens as I walk towards her again. It's almost a shame. She holds out a fresh glass of champagne with a big genuine smile on her face. At least I assume it is genuine. It's hard to tell in this company.

'You never even told me your name. Here.'

She hands me the glass. I gulp it down, determined to definitely leave this time, before my nerve turns to incoherence. But the girl grabs my arm again.

'So is it a secret or something?'

'What?'

'Your name? Or are you undercover?'

'Sorry. It's Glen and I'm leaving.'

Pulling out one of the cards I had printed but am always too embarrassed to give to anybody, I hand it to her. The girl stares at it greedily, as if there is some incredible, ultimate truth written on it.

'Glen Adamson – wow, you sound like a country singer.'

I splutter into my drink.

'Please. I prefer to think of myself as a vast, dark, imposing mountain in Sutherland. I'm more Scotland than Nashville, thanks.'

I know I'm sounding like a tosser, but only she's listening and she's lapping it up. Even so, I finish my drink and tell her I have to go.

'Aw, just stay a tiny bit longer.'

She grabs another champagne.

'Please, I wanted to ask if you would photograph me.'

I chuckle. It's out before I even think about it. The girl looks hurt.

'Sorry, but I'm not that kind of photographer. I document urban squalor, poverty, illness. I don't do weddings and pets and all that crap.'

'I can look ill. I can look poor. I'd just like some photos to take round agencies. You need photos these days. C'mon, how long would it take you? Please.'

It is definitely time to leave. What is it with women? They all seem to think they're something special. Something beautiful. I want away from this dumpy, pasty teenager. Handing her my empty glass, I push open the door.

'Keep the card. If you want to give me a phone some time I can maybe suggest people who might be interested.'

Yeah, Nigel for starters. Nigel's private web portfolio entitled 'Early Spring' might be more suitable. I don't want anything more to do with Nigel, though. He's a good guy, but shit sticks. The girl's still clinging to me. I yank myself away and out the door.

'Sorry, I'm off.'

It's raining slightly but it just feels so good to be away from that bunch of tossers, breathing fresh air. I'm conscious that I'm staggering slightly, but I still have a strong feeling of confidence, almost cockiness. My head feels like it's fizzing. It feels good. I'm ready. The time is now.

There's no sign of a taxi until I get onto the main street. It's one of the contract ones that don't usually do pick-ups but I'm not complaining. It belts through town, running red lights, flying over speed bumps on the quiet side roads. It takes six minutes to get home. Feeling shaken, but relieved, I tip the driver fifty pence.

Stumbling towards the stair door, I pause to wipe raindrops from a shop window to check my reflection. A pebble-dashed me stares back.

Sophie. Sophie. I whisper her name, breathing condensation onto the window, draw a love heart in it, then wipe it away, embarrassed with myself.

What should my first line be? Should I just come out with it? 'Sophie, we both know how we feel?' 'Both know how I feel?' 'I think we'd be good together, Sophie?' 'I want to look after you, Sophie?' 'I can't help how I feel?' No. I rehearse and reject opening lines on the way up the stairs.

The flat is empty. I knock on Sophie's bedroom door. Silence. The bathroom is empty. But Sophie said she was staying in. She was going to cook pasta if I wanted some.

There's no note, no nothing. No sign that she's cooked. I decide she must be out with somebody else. Probably that teacher guy that's been chasing her the past few months. She's finally succumbed because I didn't show for her fucking cannelloni.

My head is still fizzing, but I have this strong feeling that this is my last chance. If I don't tell her tonight I might as well forget it. It's already been a fucking year! Taking the phone through to the kitchen, I dial the mobile number on the fridge door. She answers after three. My bottle crashes simultaneously.

'Glen. Are you ok?'

I can't even manage hello. I'm hyperventilating.

'Is everything all right? Speak to me. What's wrong?'

I want to hang up. I never phone Sophie. What am I playing at? The idea she might be interested in me suddenly seems ridiculous.

'I just wondered . . . are you coming home soon . . . no . . . it's ok. Don't worry about it. Please . . . I'm sorry.'

'Has something happened? You sound upset. Tell me what's wrong, Glen. You're worrying me.'

God, get your act together, Glen, you're making a tit of yourself and scaring Sophie in the process. She's a bag of nerves at the best of times.

'Sorry Soph, I'm fine. I just . . . I've just had too much to drink. I just wanted to hear someone's voice. Really, it's ok.'

There's a pause. I imagine her telling someone on the other end that her flatmate is having a breakdown.

'Sure? I'll come home now if you like.'

This is my big chance. Seize it, seize the day.

'Naw, it's fine, honestly. I need some sleep. Really.'

'Absolutely really, babe?' She sounds relieved.

'Absolutely. I'm sorry. Can we pretend this phone call didn't happen? I'm just in a bit of a state. Didn't mean to interrupt your night.'

Another pause.

'Sure?'

'Sure. I'm going to catch some zeds.'

As soon as she hangs up, I throw the phone spinning into the living room. I feel dizzy and sick but don't know if this is down to the booze and coke or me just being a useless, cowardly, pathetic, fucking prick. Switching on the TV, I slump onto the settee and let out a groan. Eyes shut, I listen to the voices. The volume's too low to make out what they're saying but it just feels good to have someone there in the background.

The doorbell wakes me at ten the next morning. The spare duvet's over me, though I can't remember getting it out of the cupboard. I knock on Sophie's bedroom door before I answer the door to the flat. She's already left for work. The previous evening's not even had time to find its way back into my conscious thoughts when I open the door and the girl from the gallery barges in.

'I was bored, so I've come up to see what a photographer's studio's like.'

I gawp at her as she skips across the room and slumps herself down on the duvet-strewn settee. She looks about eleven. The previous night plays fast forward in my head. I didn't disgrace himself at the gallery. I phoned Sophie, but I didn't actually say what I wanted to. Did I? I just want to sit quietly and analyse the phone call. The girl pinches at the duvet.

'Did she kick you out of bed? Were you too drunk to do it?' she sniggers.

I really don't need this. I hold the door open for her to leave.

'I've got a really busy day. D'you mind?'

'Oh, c'mon, that's not very friendly. You promised to take photos of me.'

I gesture into the stair.

'I did not. I said phone me in a few weeks and I'll see if I can think of anyone. I really don't know anyone that takes these sorts of photos though. It's not my line. Come on.'

The girl crosses her arms defiantly.

'You are such a big liar. Aw go on. Just a few. I really need them. I'll love you forever, honest.'

I slam the door again, worried one of the neighbours will go past ear-wigging, and sit on the arm of the chair opposite her.

'Now look . . . what's your name again?'

'Claire. Claire Fisher. Thanks for finally asking.'

'Claire. I'm expecting someone round. I'm busy. I'm trying to make a living here.'

'How long's it gonna take, like?' she whines. 'Five minutes? Aw, go on Glen. I got you millions of champagne last night. Can't you even take a few wee photos?'

A rush of anger lifts me off my feet.

'When did you suddenly realise you suddenly needed your photos taken, like? When you saw me taking photos last night? This isn't some game. It's my job.'

She picks my Nikon off the coffee table and examines it. There's a devilment about the way she's handling it – as if she might throw it against the wall at any second.

'Ten photos. That's all I need to get the agencies interested.'

'In what, like? To do what? Model? Act? Voice-overs? Do yourself a favour, kid. Get off to school and pass some exams.'

She starts whining again. 'Please. I really need an agent. I want to be famous. I want all my pals to be famous. Christian's nice but he's not proper famous. I just need a few photos to get started, then when people see them, they'll wait outside my house to try and take photos of me.'

How foul and pathetic. Any deeply buried sympathy I had for her is extinguished. She doesn't have a hope in hell. I despise people like her. Jesus, even the youth don't have any substance left any more. It depresses me.

'The idea is, you do well at something, then, if you're very lucky, you get recognition. Not the other way round, for Christ's sake.'

'But I don't have time for all that. I'll be past it soon. I'm nearly fourteen already. Everyone I know wants the same thing. D'you know how hard that is?'

She's depressingly correct. It makes me feel ill.

'Look, I'm sorry but I can't help you. You have to leave. You're holding me back.'

Claire stays put, slapping the camera from one hand to the other.

'What if I get you work? Friends of Christian. And my brother knows a poet. And some folk in bands.'

'That's not what I do.'

I make for the door again, hoping if I open it, she'll leave. Instead, she tries to drag me back.

'Have you ever been in a tour bus? You could get great photos in a tour bus.'

She pulls me over to the settee again, simultaneously reciting some outrageous tale about having sex with two guitarists from some band I've never heard of. I feel culpable just hearing about it. She's thirteen years old for fuck's sake.

'Have you ever done coke?' she suddenly asks.

Damn that fucking Christian.

'I prefer Diet Pepsi. It's better for you.'

I fold my arms and watch in despair as she dances

round the room, bragging about taking coke with the 'band', her dad's home-grown, the eccies she necked the previous weekend, her ten Bacardi Breezers a night drink problem. The pride she obviously feels is pitiful. I tell her she shouldn't abuse her body if she seriously wants to be a model or actress. She looks at me like I'm some clueless parent.

'You don't know many supermodels then? What do you think rehab clinics are for? Imagine all the famous people you'd meet in one of them.'

She's over by the window now, striking poses. Jesus, what if Sophie comes back? She has to go.

'Look, I've had enough of this. Will you please leave? You shouldn't be here and to be honest, you're really starting to piss me off.'

'Aw, thanks a lot!' she squeals.

'C'mon, I need to take a shower. I have to be somewhere.'

'I thought you had someone coming round?'

Jesus.

'Yes, later. But I have to go somewhere first. Ok. So get out, eh.'

She stays put and pouts defiantly.

'You know what you have to do to make me leave.'

My anger is rising. It feels like it's about to boil over. I have a sense of unreality about what is happening.

'Don't try that. I'm taking no photos. Just go, please.'

'C'mon. Think about all the folk that saw us together last night. I'll tell them you invited me up here and tried it on.'

I'm stunned.

'Don't start. You latched onto me. I didn't ask you here. Stop being such a little bitch.'

'C'mon, that's not nice. You know I don't really want to do that. I just want a few photos, then I'll love you forever. Please.'

I have to take a puff on my inhaler.

'And why would I care if you loved me forever or not? I'd rather you didn't, to be honest. I might be gay for all you know.'

The idea of pretending to be bent to get rid of some deluded kid is galling but I'm getting desperate.

'Rubbish, everyone's bi these days. I saw it on the telly. Please, I don't want to tell on you. Am I ugly or something? I just want you to take my photo.'

I can't reason with her. It feels like I'm being held hostage in my own flat. I pick the Nikon up from the settee where she's left it.

'I've got six exposures left on this film. If I take six photos of you, will you promise to go away?'

Charging over, she wraps her arms around me like an over-affectionate poodle.

'I love you. I really do.'

It makes me cringe but just wanting an end to this now,

I quietly unfold a reflector, hang it beside the window and tell her to get in front of it.

'Oh wait, I have to check my face. Where's the toilet?'

I ignore her and take aim.

'You look fine. It's black and white anyway.'

But she's wandering about, looking for the toilet. I gesture to it, hopelessly but she's already sloped in and locked the door behind her. What if Sophie's just popped to the shops? It's not unknown for her to work from home. I just want to sit quietly and think about her. The bathroom door clicks open and Claire peeks round, shaking a packet of Sophie's nerve pills.

'Do these get you wasted?'

'They're my flatmate's. Just put them back and get through here.'

She dangles them like they're dirty.

'It's the pill, isn't it? Are they your girlfriend's?'

I just shrug.

'I don't bother myself. I only have sex with rich guys. That way I can't lose.'

'They're my flatmate's. Please put them back and let's get this over with, eh?'

But the door shuts and locks again and she starts shouting through to me.

'Are you rich?'

I've been self-employed for the past five years. I'm very proud of the fact that I'm now making a reasonable living, without having sold out (apart from last night). Despite this,

I tell her I'm unemployed so she doesn't get any ideas. I start banging on the bathroom door.

'Look, will you get out of there? This isn't even my flat. It's my friend, Sophie's. That's why I'm sleeping on the settee.'

Brilliant. Crashing out pissed last night could yet be my saving grace. Then I realise the address is on the business card I gave her. That's how she's here. There's a rustling sound from the bathroom.

'Ok, go over to the window and don't look till I say,' she shouts. I do as I'm told. This could all be over in five minutes. As I close my eyes and try to breathe slowly, I hear the door open and bare feet padding towards me.

'Ok, you can look now.'

The moment before I look, I have a terrifying vision of her standing naked with her arms in the air. I open my eyes. She is standing there naked with her arms in the air.

'Taa-raah!'

I scurry into the bathroom, averting my eyes. The tops are off all the perfume and aftershave bottles. Sophie's lipstick is lying crushed. There's lipstick kiss marks on the mirror. Jesus. There's an empty condom packet lying in the sink, it's blown up former inhabitant lurking in the toilet. A surge of adrenaline throws me into the rage I've been trying to suppress. Grabbing her clothes off the floor, I barge through and chuck them at her.

'Put these on and get out my fucking flat before I phone the police.'

She clucks with laughter.

'Yeah, great idea.'

Then she's over posing naked by the window, bent over, jerking like she's being taken from behind. I feel horrified and scared. Scared that if I don't get away from this soon, I'm going to lose the plot and hit her.

She walks towards me. Stops. Turns. Spreads her arse cheeks.

'C'mon. I'm ready now. Put the pictures on the internet and we can split the money. It's easy.'

I've run out of options. Running away from her, I yank open the door to the stair.

'Close up when you leave.'

I slam the door behind me and stand in a daze. Fumbling through my pockets, I find £2.97 in change and half a packet of chewing gum. My keys are in my jacket inside the flat. The thought of having to ask her to let me back in sickens me. I walk hesitantly down the stairs to the street.

The sense that I may have just made one of the biggest mistakes of my life is tempered slightly by the feeling of relief at being away from her. The growing violence in my head was terrifying me. Maybe I can just wait here for Sophie and try to explain. I try to fix on one of the hundred thoughts whizzing around my mind. Surely she'll get bored soon? She's an exhibitionist. She'll get pissed off if there's no-one to exhibit herself to. Will she trash the place? Will she stay up there till I have to go back? I've already pretended to be gay, unemployed and homeless to get rid of her.

I cross the street to the coffee shop opposite. The flat looks out to the side street but I can get a good view of the stair door to watch for her leaving or Sophie coming back. I'm so busy staring across at the door, I don't notice the assistant waiting to serve me.

'Welcome to Coffee Confidential. My name is Tracy. How can I help you?'

Asking for an espresso, I suddenly worry it will make my heart race and deepen my feeling of panic, and change it to a hot chocolate. My hands are trembling as I hand over the money and I'm sweating like a rapist. They better not call Tracy to give evidence.

Sitting by a pillar, I stare intently at the stair door opposite, willing it to open. It's only mid-morning but the traffic is distressingly heavy. She'll come out and disappear behind a bus. Sophie will sneak in without me noticing. There is a sharp pain in my temple and I fleetingly worry that my brain may be about to explode. Sophie's probably already in there. They're phoning the police together. Should I try calling from that pay phone next to the toilets? Ask to speak to Sophie, get her out of there and explain? She's probably at work. Fuck knows.

Digging a coin from my pocket, I go over to the phone and dial. It rings and rings. Relief starts to wash over me. Then she picks up.

'Glen Adamson photographer, how can I help you?'

I throw the phone down like it's burnt me. The assistant looks up. Shrugging, I sit back down with my chocolate.

This is pathetic. She can't just hold me to ransom like this. I've done nothing wrong. Why did I get those arsey cards printed in the first place? That's the first one I've actually remembered to give to anyone.

Deciding the pain in my temple is a brain tumour, I briefly take some relief from this thought. The traffic's so heavy now, I can't see a thing. A crowd could be gathering opposite, watching her spray-paint 'Glen Adamson is a beast', across my stair door. The neighbours have probably been summoned there by contrived screams.

Standing up suddenly, I knock my untouched hot chocolate onto the table. Thick brown goo starts to ooze from the gaps in the lid. Ignoring it, I burst back out onto the street. I'm just going to have to drag her out or reason with her. Coax her out in some way. Anything to get her out of there before Sophie gets home.

There's four lanes of traffic to negotiate but if I go down to the lights, I'm worried I might miss her. As I manoeuvre my way into the middle of the road, the stair door suddenly opens and the girl emerges and disappears round the corner. She looks so nonplussed, it feels like I maybe imagined it all.

The door to the flat is wide open. As I stalk in like I'm anticipating sniper fire, the room looks untouched. My jacket lies unmoved on the armchair. The keys jingle in my pocket as I pick it up, and feel my wallet in the inside pocket. My bag is unopened. The phone is lying on the settee. As I replace it on its cradle, I notice a childish scrawl on the messages pad.

'I hv ur camera 4 6 photos u o me,' and a mobile number.

I'll either have to see her again, or get a new one off the insurance but I'm too relieved to care. If I'd taken even one photo of her it would be another story, but she arsed around so much, I didn't need to. Besides, the camera was empty. Despite the temporary loss of my beloved Nikon, I feel in control again.

I go through to clean up the bathroom. It takes vinegar to get the lipstick off the mirror. As I carefully scour the rest of the flat, I realise I am surrounded by things I haven't noticed for months. It's not like she's moved them. Just that I haven't looked since I first laid them down – bills, concert tickets, invoices, books seem to cover every surface. I feel embarrassed by my mess and try to clean up as I look around in vain for anything that might not be there any more.

I leave Sophie's room till last. Sophie sees her room as her sanctuary and although I'm totally respectful of that, I have to check.

The sight of the unmade bed and one of the pillows on the floor totally unnerves me. I can't imagine Sophie leaving a mess like that. She always seems so immaculate. Then again, if she was that fastidious, how could she stand to share with an untidy bastard like me?

I pick up the discarded pillows, then fluff up the duvet,

throw it on the bed and smooth down the sides. As I stand and stare at the bed, I can smell Sophie's smell. An exotic, musky clinging sort of sweetness. It permeates the whole room. I inhale, imagining myself nuzzling into her hair, feeling her softness and warmth. I have to drag myself away. The door to my own room is still locked. I can't remember why I locked it but again, feel I have done the right thing without knowing why.

When Sophie comes home at 3.15, I'm crashed in front of the telly. I hate watching telly usually. My raison d'etre is to document life, not watch other people's limp interpretations of it.

'Didn't you have a job on this afternoon, babe?' she asks as she fumbles with the remote to turn the volume down. I hadn't noticed how loud it was. 'Are you ok? You sounded strange last night. What did you want to tell me?'

'Nothing, honestly. I've left my camera somewhere. I've been through the flat. It's not here. I was just upset.'

'What, your Nikon? Did you have it with you last night? Have you tried the gallery? Christ!'

'They said they'd phone if anything turned up. I think I've had it though.'

Sophie doesn't look convinced. I am forever telling her that me and my Nikon are inseparable. It is my eyes to the world. Once, when I was drunk, I told her emphatically that it was the love of my life. That was one of my earlier attempts at telling Sophie how I felt about her. Sophie takes her briefcase through to her room. Everything seems to stop. I expect her to come stomping back through and accuse me of something but she shuts the door behind her.

I take the girl's crumpled message out of my pocket and look at it again. I walk over to the window and imagine her being out there somewhere, telling people God knows what about me. I think about Rick in Somalia and briefly hope he stands on a landmine for being the cause of all this in the first place. I toy with the idea of going to the gallery and telling them my camera was stolen. Then if that little tart starts flashing it around, they'll think it was her. This idea is quickly discarded though. She could be the daughter of the gallery proprietor for all I know. Opening the window and jumping out, three floors down into the boxes of fruit and veg outside the grocers below suddenly seems more realistic. Maybe I should go away for a few days. I've found, by experience, that running away is usually the answer. I have been running away since I was a kid.

I hear Sophie's door opening. My insides are knotted and sore. I just want to tell her what happened and ask her what I should do and throw myself into her arms, but it all sounds so fucking ridiculous.

'Glen, have you been in my room?'

I mean to say yes, but I'm terrified. What's that little bitch done in there?

'Er, no. You know I wouldn't go in your room.'

Sophie gives me another chance.

'Oh. I just thought you might have looked in when you were trying to find your camera.'

Despite the fact I'm lying, I feel offended.

'Why would it be in there? You know I don't go in your room, Sophie. Why?'

Sophie wags her hands in front of her.

'Sorry babe. It's just me. Ignore me, please. I think I'm working too hard. Or playing too hard. One or the other.'

She grins an apology and goes to put the kettle on. I know I should feel relieved. It was obviously just the bed. She didn't make it this morning, but now thinks she must have. I was right to act offended. Playing too hard though? What does she mean by that? Where was she last night, and with who? Was it that teacher guy? Did she fuck him? Were they fucking when I phoned? I try to remember what she said, and how she sounded when we spoke. Did she break off mid-fuck to have me talk shit to her? I follow her through to the kitchen.

'How was your night? You must have been late.'

Sophie's smile confirms all my fears. It says, don't ask, but I have a beautiful secret. I've pissed about the bush for too long and now it's too late. I want to slap her.

'How about you? Sounded like the gallery didn't go too well. D'you think someone stole your camera?'

'I don't bloody know. You know I never put it down. Unless they took it out of my bag while it was strapped to me.'

Sophie starts searching under the settee, behind the chair, round all the shelves.

'It's no good. I've looked. I have the film from last night, but my Nikon's vanished.'

Sophie shrugs.

'Were you with anyone? Did you go for a drink afterwards? Maybe they've picked it up.'

I feign offence.

'Like I hang around with arseholes like that, Soph. You know me. These people make me sick. I just came straight home, realised I'd lost it, phoned you and crashed out.'

'I don't know then. Try the gallery again. Maybe you left it in a taxi. I'm knackered, to be honest. I'm going to have a shower to freshen myself up.'

I'm relieved. She's not giving me time to think. I'm worried I'll trip myself up. Sophie disappears into the bathroom and I hear the shower go on. I take out the cafetiere and spoon coffee into it from the packet. As the kettle clicks off, I hear knocking at the flat door. I seize up. Hoping Sophie won't have heard it for the shower, I ignore it. She comes out of the bathroom in her robe, confused.

'Aren't you going to get that?'

'What?'

Sophie shakes her head and goes to answer it.

'What is up with you, Glen? I heard it in the bathroom.'

I'm cowering at the kitchen door with the packet of coffee still in my hand when the girl walks in with the camera. Sophie gestures to her.

'There you go. He's been wondering what he did with

that. Did he leave it at the gallery? They said they didn't have it when he phoned,' she says, inviting the girl in. I can't move.

The girl gawps at Sophie's robe as she hands her the camera.

'I take it you're Sophie.'

Sophie looks at me, then back at the girl.

'Yes, and you are . . . since Glen's being a bit lapse with the introductions.'

The girl gives Sophie a wave.

'I'm Claire. Claire Fisher. Hasn't Glen mentioned me to you yet? He promised he would. Maybe he's ashamed of me. Are you, Glen?'

The two women stare at me for a response. Sophie sits down on the arm of the chair, not taking her eyes off me.

'Glen?'

I feel empty. I have lost the ability to speak and I feel empty and guilty. The girl walks up and puts her hand on my shoulder.

'Tell her Glen, please. You said she'd understand. Please, I thought you loved me.'

Sophie's jaw drops open. Her eyes seem to glaze over. I push the girl away and stand up. My mouth starts working of its own accord.

'Sophie, really. I'm sorry. This is a load of shit. She's thirteen.'

The girl humphs.

'That didn't seem to matter when I was naked.'

Glen moves towards Sophie, pleading, 'I didn't ask her to take her clothes off, honestly. It wasn't my fault, Sophie. Please understand.'

Sophie storms into my room. I hear banging about and the sound of her breathing and sighing. Coming back through with my two holdalls, she throws them across the room at me.

'Just get out of my house. Please, I don't want to hear any more. You've got fifteen minutes then I'm phoning the police, so please just pack and get out.'

She picks up the bags, throws them again then looks at her watch.

'Fourteen minutes.'

'Please, Sophie. It's not like that. I wanted to tell you.'

She can't seem to hear me for her own thoughts.

'Jesus, your orphans and your children's wards and your refugee kids. Eugh, Christ. You make me sick. In my flat! In MY flat!'

I still can't move. Sophie blusters back to my room again and starts throwing my stuff out the door. Even the girl is looking concerned. She starts pleading with Sophie.

'I know he's leaving soon, but don't chuck him out yet. Please, it was just the once. He's nice, really. It's all my fault.'

Sophie reappears and throws my ghetto blaster at me.

'Please, just get out. And keep away from her. You've

twisted her mind already. Listen to her. Jesus. I always thought there was something creepy about you, Glen, but Jesus, not this.'

I begin stuffing the growing pile of clothes into the larger of the holdalls. There's no explaining with that little bitch here. After all the shit earlier, I know I have no hope of getting her out unless I go too. She tries to help me but I push her out of the way.

'Please don't come near me. Please go away.'

I stuff what I can in the two holdalls and park them at the flat door. The girl is sitting on the arm of the chair now, watching me like it's all a big joke. I go through to Sophie again. She's stopped going through my stuff and is sitting on the end of my bed, crying.

'Sophie, believe me. This isn't how it seems. She wants me to take her photo and she's just doing this to hurt me because I won't.'

Sophie stands up. Even with red eyes and a snotty nose, she is the most beautiful creature I've ever seen.

'I told you about me and my stepdad, for fuck's sake,' she whispers. 'I thought you were a good person.'

I try to console her.

'I am a good person, Soph. You know I am. I'll phone in a few days and explain. You'll understand.'

Punching me on the head, she heads for the phone.

'Nah, that's it. If I let you walk away, I'm as bad as you.'

She picks up the receiver and pushes in the first 9.

The girl grabs the smaller of the holdalls and opens the door to the flat.

'Come on, Glen. She's just jealous and stuck-up. She'll never understand.'

Sophie stares at me and pushes the second 9.

'Are you going or not? Last chance. I don't particularly want people pointing at me saying, "There's that girl that lived with the paedophile." But if I have to, I will.'

I pick up the larger holdall and open the flat door. It feels like it is full of bricks.

'Just believe me, Sophie. One day you will understand,' I manage to say before she flies across the room and slams me out into the stair. The girl is standing beside me, smiling and gripping onto my other bag. Yanking it off her, I storm down the stairs with the sound of her feet padding after me.

'Come on, Glen, we can be friends now.'

The big holdall is too heavy so I kick it down the stairs in front of me, then drag it out onto the street. It feels incredible to be out amidst sanity, cars, shops, people. Despite having done nothing wrong, I suddenly feel like I've got away with something. Stopping a taxi, I manage to climb in just as the girl catches up with me. I slam the door behind me.

'Where you going, mate?'

Claire bangs on the window and tries the door, but the driver's already put on the safety lock.

I point ahead but don't have a clue.

Meat

I'VE JUST GONE to bed when I hear them come staggering back from their quiz night at the local pub. This is the last thing I need.

'I saw you, Ewan. All over her!'

'Ocht, can we no leave the house without you going radge? Just once?'

'You're no denying it then?'

'Shuttup woman!'

'You get a kick out of humiliating me, don't you?'

'What are you on about?'

'That wee slapper in the black dress you couldnae take your eyes off. Slobbering over her like a dug in heat.'

'Loady shite!'

'"*Can I join YOUR team? Mind if I join YOUR team?*" She was lapping it up. Dirty wee hoor.'

My father's responses become shorter and quieter until eventually my mother's grievances are a capella. It's always the same when she gets angry. Her voice takes on this unbearably shrill working class tone that could shatter windows within a fifty foot radius.

'Go your fucking self next week. I'm not going back after that. How would you like it if I threw myself at any man that came within a foot of me? You want to start playing games like that? D'you? D'you? Think I've no had my chances, eh? D'you?'

Her insults, as ever, are interspersed with the sounds of slapping and banging around. I know Dad'll just be sitting there, taking it like he always does.

Quite when my father is meant to conduct all his supposed affairs is beyond me. When he's not at work the pair of them are never out of each other's pockets. Besides, he's a sap. That's probably why she loves him. One day he'll maybe snap and shag someone else but I doubt it.

Eventually I hear her stumbling up the stairs and going into their bedroom. A few minutes later he follows her up and opens my door. He stands in the darkness, hiding, then tiptoes over and sits on the side of my bed.

'I'm sorry son. Are you sleeping? You shouldnae have to listen to that.' I simulate light snoring to save him his embarrassment.

'Go and come fishing with me tomorrow, give me a wee break. You used to like it. We dinnae spend enough time together.'

This is very true but I still don't move.

'Duncan's boat's at Dysart. If we leave early we can dig some bait at Cramond and get across before the tide goes out.'

Where the fuck is Dysart? My father doesn't half go to some wee-arsed places.

'It's up to you, but. Give us a chance to have that wee talk you mentioned. I winnae let you down again, honest.'

The fact is, he never lets me down deliberately. He needs the overtime, we all do. It's years since we've been fishing together and I can't even remember if I liked it or not. We really do need to talk but the thought of being stranded alone with him for hours makes me a bit edgy. He's standing beside the bed now. Either he knows I'm awake or he just wants to hide for a wee while longer. I can't pretend any more, I feel so sorry for him.

'Aye Dad, I'd like that.'

As he ruffles the blanket over my head like I'm still a wee laddie I take advantage of his moment of paternal joy and ask him for a loan of a tenner. He gladly hands me a note from his pocket then goes off to his bed, smiling, partially rejuvenated. If only I could be as easily satisfied. Parents get so much out of the few crumbs of affection you throw them.

That night I have a wet dream about Mum. I come all over her face. She gets up to make us a packed lunch and cook breakfast at 7.15, the sleep having returned her to her normal, prudish, pseudo-middle class self again, but I can't look at her and just grunt when she tries to talk to me. Maybe she'll think I've taken the huff about their fight last night. I hope she does as it might make her a bit easier on the poor old sod.

We arrive at Cramond at 8.30. Dad makes me take my Walkman out with us as it's supposedly a bad place for cars being broken into. The tide's beginning to come in and the oily beach is leopard-printed with pools of water. We walk from the dry, stony littery sandy grass onto the soft blackened beach which clutches at our feet as we progress. Jumbo jets roar past overhead as they drop into Turnhouse.

A group of teenage boys swaggers down the walkway from the island, swearing and sniggering and reeking of bad vibes. Dad puts his head down in the way people do to fruitlessly avoid being noticed and walks purposefully down the beach a few feet in front of me. As the teenagers approach, they try to get our attention. Dad continues walking, having switched off in the same way he does when Mum throws one of her wobblies. The hostile noises get louder but they're still too far away for us to make out what they're saying. I feel scared and scan the deserted beach for allies in case of attack. There's only an old woman walking her dog up towards where we left the car. She doesn't look like she'll do us many favours in a fight. The tallest of the boys now stands parallel with Dad and waves.

'Hoi, Grandad. How'd ye get ti Barnton from here?'

Dad remains impervious. I want to panel the guy for calling my father Grandad but I'm way too feart.

'Hoi Grandad, hoi mate.'

He looks around.

'Barnton, Grandad. What direction?'

Dad gestures upwards noncommittally and the dirty-looking group continues past us and up the beach, the tallest one muttering loudly, 'It fuckin' better be or we'll come back and chib yi, yi cunt.'

I glance back a few times as we continue down the beach until I see them pass the car, leaving the windscreen intact, and disappear up the street. Dad stops in front of me, draws a circle in the sand with his garden fork and begins digging.

'Here, get they twa big soosters in that bucket,' he says, pointing at two of the biggest, most deformed-looking worms I've ever seen outside a reality TV programme. I feel nauseated at first but once I actually pick them up and feel their sliminess in my hand it transports me back to being eight years old, cutting them into dozens of pieces in our garden and watching them slithering around like maggots just prior to putting them down the wee girl next door's dress.

I begin filling the bucket with the fat-necked monsters as Dad spins about the beach drawing his circles and digging vigorously. My eyes take a while to adjust to the camouflage of their gritty bodies and Dad has to keep prompting me to grab them before they take fright and disappear back into the sand. I watch the poor bugger dig out about fifteen circles before volunteering to dig myself. The sweat is out on his forehead but he looks like he's enjoying himself.

He points out that I should dig where the craters are and not over the piles of sand worms which I'd thought more likely to signal their location. The sand is wet and heavy and I'm panting whilst still digging out my first circle as it's hard to move before it escapes through the spaces in the fork. Since Dad makes it look so simple though, I persevere, but I'm too embarrassed to ask how to do it properly. I can't find any of the fat wee bastards he's been unearthing and after three lacklustre circles have only managed to collect two the size of earwigs and I'm completely knackered. Dad sees that I'm suffering, dips the bucket into a pool of water and chucks in some sand.

'That'll do for now. The tide'll be out by the time we get over,' he says, nodding sentimentally in the general direction of his beloved Fife.

As we drive onto the Forth Road Bridge I realise this'll be the first time I've been outside Edinburgh since I was ten. The guy I call Uncle went through a brief stage of taking me to the stock-car racing in Newtongrange a couple of years ago but that doesn't really count because it's still sort of Edinburgh and I found it really boring. We haven't been on an actual holiday since my first and last visit to London in 1990. The IRA waited until we arrived, then bombed the City and blew up some Tory outside the Houses of Parliament all during our fortnight there. The police kept cordoning off the streets and tube stations because of bomb scares and it seemed like the most exciting place in the world to be. For a short time after that Mum and Dad would occasionally discuss where our next holiday would be, but that next holiday never happened and eventually the whole subject of holidays was dropped and never mentioned again.

So although an afternoon's fishing with Dad is certainly not my idea of fun, at least it feels like I'm escaping for a little while. I'm not even sure if I'm going to mention my situation to him now. Maybe it would be nice to just forget about it for a day.

It takes about forty minutes to reach the picture postcard wee harbour. Dad struggles into his waders as I transfer the equipment from the car into Duncan's boat. It's only a seventeen-footer but there's a couple of bunks and, thankfully, a small engine. At least I won't get lumbered with all the rowing like I used to when we fished the lochs when I was wee.

Dad manoeuvres the boat down the slipway, wading slowly around to the bow until the sea is up to his chest. As I stand feeling decidedly useless and clumsy, I worry that he'll slip on the seaweed he warned me about and split his head open. I'm sure he must know what he's doing but it looks terribly complicated and I wish we could just get on with it. I watch him undo the straps that harness the trailer to the boat and try to push the undercarriage up the slipway before my impatience finally gets the better of me. I grab hold and help him pull it back up, securing the wheels with a couple of bricks. It never dawned on me that all this palaver would be required to get a boat into the sea. I always assumed you just dropped them over the side of the harbour wall and they landed the right way up.

As Dad finally pulls the boat clear of the slipway he gets in and shouts me over to the ladder at the side of the jetty. I climb down and jump in, feeling almost excited. Dad yanks the engine cord and we splutter past the breakwater into the seemingly vast expanse of the Forth. It's 10.15 on a Sunday morning, the sun is glinting off the waves and I start to see why he makes such a fuss about sea fishing. It's like we're sitting on top of the world.

My initial feelings of nausea as I get used to the bobbing are soon surpassed by a sort of calm, excited contentment. Leaning my head back, I trail my fingers in the warm sea as we rock towards Seafield Tower.

We stop near a buoy and let the boat drift. Dad stands behind me and demonstrates how to drop the line and reel it in. It feels more like proper fishing than casting, which I used to be terrible at. I enjoy the unusual sensation of having my father's arms around me as he tries to show me how to tell when the line has hit the sea bed. My smooth, waxen fingers look feminine cradled in his rough, powerful hands. I don't care about fishing, I just want him to hold me. A strong sense that this is my father and I am his son makes me feel incredibly safe and untouchable as I watch the worm's blood rolling along the groove at the side of the boat.

Dad tries to make our hooks irresistible by loading his homemade mackerel flies with generous helpings of the serpents he dug earlier. Before long my rod is jerking in appreciation, not with mackerel but cod. It's not a long struggle like trying to land a trout. I just reel in, Dad unhooks the fish and chucks it at the crate inside the boat. The first one is still slapping about in disbelief when we throw the second and third in. You'd think they'd just give up after a while but they seem to take hours to die.

We catch so many in the initial flurry; I suspect Jesus has walked past on the water while my mind was elsewhere. Any smaller than a pound, we use as bait, or slit open and lob into the air, to be gulped down whole by seagulls in flight.

'Bet if we threw them chunks of us, they'd eat that too,' says Dad, the sea air making him momentarily profound. He's right, though. We're all just part of the same huge food chain.

I lose all sense of time. Hours fly by unnoticed. Dad's glowing, delighted to be fishing with his 'boy' again. He looks like he does in old photos. His face is relaxed, not screwed-up in frustration like usual and his wrinkles seem to have vanished. I can't shatter all that. Then again, while he's oozing with paternal goodwill like this, it's probably the perfect time.

Taking my rod, he trawls our lines behind the boat and brings the lunch bag from the cabin. How come tomato and chopped pork rolls taste so good in the outdoors? I wouldn't touch them in any other circumstances. As we share the flask top of coffee, Dad puts his arm round me, and points at a seal. It takes me a while to make it out amidst the grey choppy sea and fog that's starting to steam off the waves. By the time I've manage to focus, Dad's attention has moved to a family of puffins bobbing past on the other side.

He notices things nobody else does – birdcalls, the names of different types of mushrooms, which animals do which droppings, birds sleeping in bushes. Even if it's just a way of avoiding talking about real things, it must make him more likely to understand. I don't mean for him to tell Mum. I just want to give him the chance to know me like he knows his animals and plants.

'Looking awfie deep in thought there. Bit of a dreamer like me, eh?'

I have to say something.

'Know Shirley, Dad?' Shirley's my best pal. She likes it on the scene because guys don't hassle her. She chummed me for the test. Dad likes her.

'Aye, super lassie. You couldn't have done better.'

Shit. What does he think I'm about to tell him? I've always assumed he knew we were just friends but I suppose it could look like more. We see so much of each other and I've never bothered to explain otherwise.

'Naw Dad, this isn't exactly about Shirley. Well, she sort of knows and that but I just mentioned her so you'd know she knows, y'know, and she's ok about it . . .'

My tongue is tripping me. The part of my brain that forms coherent sentences has packed in.

'Get engaged. Why not? You don't need to play the mine-field.' He laughs at his attempted joke. 'Look at me and Mum. She was my first proper girlfriend and we're ok.'

Now he is joking? Him and Mum, ok? Does he really enjoy his every utterance being shouted down or snapped at? Is that why Mum's so bored, she knocks herself out with Diazepam and goes to bed at half-seven every night? He's right. They truly are a wonderful advert for getting hitched.

'Or get a flat together, when you get your degree. Mum and me have a bit of money stashed for when you get married. You dinnae need some bit paper, if you're happy, anyway, though.'

'Naw Dad. It's not like that. We're not going out together. She's just a pal. Seriously.'

He grins.

'Don't be embarrassed. Mum doesnae mind. She's hardly a prude, y'know?

'Dad, please, listen. Shirley's my friend. Just my friend.'

'Rubbish. Stunner like that? You'd have to be bent not to fancy that.'

The very idea makes him guffaw.

'I am, Dad.'

It comes out so quiet I'm not sure he's heard me. His smile remains fixed but his eyes say it all. I think I see the wrinkles breaking out again. I wait for him to cry, or scream or throw me overboard but he turns around, as if nothing has happened, and reels in his line.

'It's getting dark. Better get our gubbins together.'

He starts clearing up – dismantling rods, putting the flask in the bag, not looking at, or acknowledging me. I try to help but he pushes me away. Emptying and rinsing the bait bucket, he throws it, clattering, into the cabin. The harsh, loud noise makes me jump.

'Did you hear what I said, Dad?'

'Loud and clear.'

Tugging on the engine cord until chugging drowns out any other attempt at conversation, he glares straight ahead as he guides us back towards the harbour. I sit in shock.

By the time we get the boat back up the slipway and transfer our stuff to the car, the fog is thick and it's starting to get dark. Aside from a few shouted orders on the boat, nothing further has been said. Getting in the car, we pull out of Dysart onto country roads. As we came here on the motorway, though, I'm not sure where we're heading.

'Is this a different way back?'

'Aye,' he barks.

I've not seen him this close to losing it since the time he found out one of his pals from school had been drowned while she was on holiday. It's the only time I've ever seen him cry. He seemed to cry for days. It was years ago, but I still remember feeling really scared, because Dad suddenly wasn't in control. Like now.

'Why are we going this way?'

'I don't bloody know.'

The fog gets worse as we manoeuvre our way round winding roads, barely wider than the car itself. It's impossible to see further than a few feet ahead. Dad's doing forty miles an hour though, cursing each time we mount the grassy verge on corners. Are we even going in the right direction? Why won't he say something? I have so much more to tell him. We're going to end up wrapped round a tree at this rate.

'Dad, please. Go back on the motorway. It's dangerous here. You can't see where you're going.'

'I've driven in fog before.'

Suddenly, out of nowhere, the headlights pick out something on the road.

I let out an embarrassingly effeminate shriek as the car veers off to the left and slams against a fence. I lurch against my seatbelt. When I come to, Dad's hyperventilating, glowering at the dashboard as if it's somehow to blame. I lean over to check he's all right but he yanks himself away and lunges out of the car.

By the time I catch up with him he's kneeling in the middle of the road, hugging a shapeless bundle. In the little light left, it looks like a bag of shopping. Reaching down to touch sticky, matted wool, though, I realise it's a lamb. My fingers slip into some slimy, unseen gash. It makes me squeal. Dad responds with a look of disgust as I wipe its syrupy blood onto my trousers. It smells like a butcher shop on a hot day. Jesus, don't let me be sick.

'Is it dead? What'll we do with it?'

Dad looks down at it and smiles.

'Know how much these things are worth? Know how much meat you get off a wee thing like this? There better be plenty room in the freezer.'

Staggering back to the car, the animal weighing his body into a slouch, he puts the still warm body in the boot. Hopefully, it died before it had time to register the pain. I wonder if its parents are looking for it.

Thankfully, Dad decides to go back on the motorway. He's persisting with the strong, silent crap, though, so I just watch Fife scooting past, through the window.

'Dad, about what I said. Can't we t . . .'

'You've told me, all right?'

North Queensferry is reached in silence. Just as we get back onto the Bridge, though, the car starts shuddering and banging, as if the engine's about to explode. The shock makes Dad swerve slightly, into the path of a massive, speeding juggernaut, which only just misses us, horn blaring. I want us to stop but the traffic heading into Edinburgh is so heavy, it's impossible. It sounds like someone's shooting at us. Jesus. The car's going to blow up, if one of us doesn't beat it to it.

'What is it? Is it the engine? Has it happened before?' I ramble, as the clattering seems to get louder. Then I realise he's sitting there laughing. Laughing at me.

'It's our friend.'

'How d'you mean?'

'That bugger. Rumours of his death have been greatly exaggerated.'

I think he's getting some dig at me, then realise he means the lamb. He's right. It's coming from the boot. At least they don't have toll booths any more. God knows what they'd make of it. There's brief lulls then it starts up again, demented drumming and the most awful wailing. It sounds more like a whale mourning a dead partner on a beach, than a half-dead lamb. Dad still finds it hilarious, though.

'What'll we do with it? Mum won't let us keep a sheep in the back garden.'

He sneers at me.

'I wasn't planning on making friends with it. I'll kill it. Lamb chops till Christmas.'

'Kill it? But it's survived. You can't do that.'

'Oh, dinnae be so bloody wet. If we'd knocked it down and killed it, that would have been fine, like?'

'Ay, but that was an accident. What are you going to do, poison it?'

Dad's laughing again, not in the warm way he usually laughs but in a malevolent, unhinged sort of way that makes me shudder.

'Clunk it on the head. What d'you think? It'll probably bleed to death by the time we get home, anyway.'

I feel sick. The mewling sound is going right through me. I keep imagining the poor wee thing, spending its dying minutes, scared, in agony, confused and alone in the petrol-smelling boot of a strange car. Dad's less concerned.

'Shut up back there. Can you not die with some dignity?'

Is this sudden macho shit for my benefit? I'm gay because he's too sensitive? If he acts like a hard hetero for five minutes after seventeen years, I'll be cured? He doesn't even know what's wrong with me. What's really wrong.

As we drive past a bus stop on Calder Road, I'm sure a few people hear the commotion. Someone's going to phone the police with our registration number. How can a half-dead creature make so much noise? We'll never get it out of the boot if it's having convulsions like this.

When we finally pull into our street, it's been raining and the neighbours' two boys are kicking a muddy cushion about. Dad makes me get out to open the garage. The kids follow me.

'That's some fucking old banger, Mr Frazer. Can you no afford a real engine?'

I try to ignore them as I wait for Dad, but they're still going on when he slams the garage door shut.

'What's in the boot, Mr Frazer? You kidnapped some-one's wean? They let Mrs Frazer out for the day wi'out her straitjacket?'

Dad blanks them and goes to the kitchen to tell Mum about the invalid. I stand and wait for him in the living room. I just sense that this is not over yet. Ages seem to pass. What if he's telling her about me? Surely not. Mum's hated poofs since a teacher interfered with her friend's wee boy. She thinks gay equals paedophile. He won't have the nerve to tell her. Besides, they never talk about important things. Just *National Geographic* monologues from him and snidey comments from her.

I can hear the lamb bleating, faintly, as I stare at a photo of Eddie, Mum's brother. If they only knew the half of it. Dad comes back through and makes me follow him to the garage. I try to sense if Mum seems different towards me as I pass her in the kitchen but she's only interested in the imminent free meat. Naturally, that's much more important than me, than my life.

'Shouldn't you take it to a butchers to chop up? You don't know what bits are edible, Ewan. It's maybe full of disease.'

When Dad eventually opens the boot, the combined stench of blood, piss, fish and dung is overwhelming. It makes my eyes sting. It squeezes my windpipe and I have to puke on the concrete. The lamb, still mewing, pathetically, has rolled onto its back and become wedged between our debris and the fishing bag. One of its front legs is bent up the wrong way. I don't know if this happened when we knocked it down, or if we shut the boot on it. Splintered bone juts out at the back of the knee. Its matted fur is caked, purple and black. One whiff is enough to send Mum back into the house with a tea towel over her face. Whether this is to block out the smell or the carnage, I'm not sure. It's way past her bedtime, anyway.

Dad picks an oily sheet from the ground and wraps it round the lamb. It starts squawking like a car alarm. It's painful to listen to. I realise it has an ear missing. The car must have wrenched it off. Part of the skull is gone and there's pinkish, grey blubber, oozing from the wound. How is it still alive?

Its awful crying gets louder as Dad tries to take it out of the car. Its three good legs wriggle frantically, like a cartoon character running, as it tries to find the ground. Its bad leg is up in front of it, like it's pleading with us to stop.

Dad makes me hold it as he searches for something to carry out the execution with – the axe, some cheesewire, a saw, the Stanley knife? He settles for a hammer and starts swinging it about at his side, grunting and pulling weird faces like a Maori warrior. It's so not Dad, it's scary.

The lamb takes fright as well, losing control of its bladder and soaking my jeans with hot, bloody piss. But I can't let go of it, even though it's skittery and the more it struggles, the more it slobbers and bleeds on me. Several times, I have to swallow my own sick. I feel like I'm going to choke. I'm trying to block out what's happening but it's difficult with something dying in agony in my arms.

Dad tells me to grab it and keep its head steady. I'm hating it, but I try to think of it as putting an end to its suffering. I have to.

'There, yeah, right there,' he growls, pornographically.

The animal, sensing it's about to die, starts wriggling more than ever. It refuses to stop fighting. Then suddenly the hammer is down, just missing me. The lamb roars as the edge of the metal ball splits its eyeball apart. Fresh blood sprays my face and open mouth. But the struggling has stopped. We both look down at the wet pool that was once an eye. I loosen my grip to let it fall to the ground, but the remaining eyelid flickers and it wheezes out another agonised meheheheheh.

'Again, again. Do it again,' I shout, grabbing it back and offering its head for another whacking. I'm hardening to the awfulness of it. There's no option. I brace myself for the next impact, but Dad just stands there, trembling.

'Come on, do it, now . . . now. Christ c'mon.'

It lets out another tragic bleat and I look up at Dad, who's started sobbing.

Dropping the hammer onto the concrete, he runs out of the garage, leaving me with the stunned creature burring and haemorrhaging on my lap. I stroke the sticky, wheezing bundle, as I wait for him to reappear.

He doesn't come back. It was his fault, but he's left me to sort it out. I went out today, hoping for support, but instead I'm the one that has to be strong. It suddenly feels like the lamb and me are the only living things left on the planet. We've been left alone to die together.

Wrapping the oily sheet round it, I put it back in the boot, removing the fishing bag and tackle to give it more room. Its eye is still bleeding but the gash on its head has congealed. It's too weak to bleat any more. There's only a wheezing kind of death rattle coming from it now. If I close the boot it'll probably die anyway but it just seems so helpless and desperate, I can't bring myself to.

This time last week, everything was fine. The lamb was probably scampering round a field, chewing grass and doing whatever it is lambs do. I was doing whatever it was I used to do, thinking I would live forever. Now look at the pair of us.

Picking up the hammer off the concrete, I apologise and take aim.